The Knights Of Freedom

Second Edition

A sequel to THE KING MAKER

by

Ben Reinhart

Acknowledgments

To my mom, who at 94 took the time to edit both of my books.
and tell me where it needed improvement.

To my awesome 16-year-old grandson
Dylan Reinhart,
who wrote chapter 16 and directed
the creation of several other chapters

To my excellent proofreader
Dusty George
who makes me look good

Disclaimer

The names of real-life organizations that may coincide with names of groups noted in this book are purely coincidental and are not intended to reflect any of these groups' beliefs or philosophies. Likewise, any real-life existence of groups noted in this book are not an endorsement or recognition of such groups.

This book is completely fictional and is intended to be nothing more than entertainment to the reader.

This story is a work of fiction. Names, characters, businesses, places, events, locales, and incidents are either the products of the author's imagination or used in a fictitious manner. Any resemblance to actual persons, living or dead, or actual organizations or events is purely coincidental.

TABLE OF CONTENTS

The "King Maker" Trilogy

Book 1 .... The King Maker

Book 2 .... The Knights of Freedom

Book 3 .... The Winds of Change

Look for more books in this series at

www.BenReinhartBooks.com

Prologue

Just over three years ago, the turning basin at Port Everglades, Florida, was completely engulfed in fire. Several explosions had occurred on the world's largest cruise ship as it entered the port causing an inferno unlike anything seen before. These explosions broke the ship in two and resulted in dozens of smaller cruise ships moored at adjacent docks to catch fire.

For weeks, television sets around the world showed the Emerald Green, or what remained of it, broken in half with its bow fully submerged in the turning basin's forty feet of murky water. Thousands of whole and partial bodies were seen being carried out to sea as the tide created a powerful current exiting the inlet. News footage was showing sharks gathering just outside the inlet that were feasting on corpses and body parts. The public bore witness to this feeding frenzy.

According to one news report, the death toll from the three explosions far exceeded four thousand vacationing families and crew. In terms of lives lost and financial impact, it was the largest terrorist attack ever within the United States of America.

Bill McPherson, President of the United States, knew a retaliation against the Syrian led New Muslim World Order (NMWO), who many blamed for this disaster, was necessary. However, it would be nothing more than a political stunt he hoped would keep his adversaries from demanding his resignation.

In a necessary calculated response by the United States government, seven Predator MQ-9 drones and sixteen cruise missiles each hit their targets within Syria.

McPherson also ordered additional bombings from a supersonic B-1 heavy bomber called the "Bone" *(from "B-One")* and a newer B-61 stealth bomber.

However, the cause of this disaster was not foreign terrorists, but rather a terrorist attack by a subversive group within the United States. The goal of this group was to show that the current U.S. government was weak and leaderless.

This group, known as *The Knights of Freedom*, with the help of Congress, created several new Amendments to the U.S.

Constitution and was only a few months away from seeing these amendments ratified by the States.

Bill McPherson's retaliation against Syria, however, was not the only duping of the American public.

We now know the plane of the Secret Service agent who exposed this group to the world did not disappear in the Bermuda Triangle as reported by the news. This also was a brilliantly executed hoax.

What really did happen, and Bill McPherson was among only a few who knew, was Jason Williams and his ex-wife Christine boarded a different jet which was hidden in the hangar at Ft. Lauderdale's Executive Airport and retreated into exile deep inside Cuba.

Their secret and well-organized plan gave them the opportunity to live without fear of retribution from *The Knights of Freedom*, the group that was determined to find and terminate this man who exposed them and their plan to the world.

Jason and his ex-wife Christine remarried and were happy living in exile in Cuba. The hacienda Jason had acquired was just west of the United States military base at Guantanamo. It was a three-acre property which sat directly on the Caribbean Sea. Aside from the beautiful views, part of the decision to acquire this property was its high level of security and privacy.

While in exile, there had already been two attempts on his son Justin's life back in New York and one on his oldest daughter, Tonya, who had been involved in a suspicious hit-and-run accident that left her paralyzed for almost a year.

Her younger sister Teresa, who Tonya watched over because of her out-of-control gambling habits, lost Tonya's help and support, due to the rehabilitation that was needed. Without support, Teresa returned to her old gambling habits.

At some point in time, Jason knew he'd have to return to the United States, but until then, he just wanted to be happy and be with Christine. He knew *The Knights of Freedom* would eventually come looking for him once they found out he was still alive.

Chapter 1 – Unexpected Visitors

Hurricane Emily, forecast to be a category-five storm, was now a category-three and had just crossed the Leeward Islands southeast of Cuba. She was expected to turn northwest and head directly toward the island of Cuba, arriving there within the next twenty-four hours. They expected her to hit somewhere on the island of Cuba as a Cat-5 storm.

However, today was just another end-of-summer day on the island, which began with a warm Caribbean breeze blowing from the east end of the island toward the west. The afternoon was just beginning to drag on as the sun started its descent.

A few miles away, in preparation for a kidnapping assault on a secure hacienda, three men and one woman could be seen loading a twenty-eight-foot open-fisherman with ammo, several semi-automatic AK-47's, some stun-guns, a few handguns, and a couple of green camouflage jumpsuits.

Two of the gunmen were Cubans with long unmanaged beards. They were tall and well built. The third gunman, an American, was younger and skinnier with a well maintained thin, charismatic beard. He looked the lover type and was rumored to be an offspring of the fourth person, an American woman, and owner of the Tat-II.

The boat's owner, Traycia Torres, was the illegitimate daughter of Cuban drug lord, Ronaldo Torres. Ronaldo happened to spend one drunken night with Traycia's mother who was undercover and working with the DEA. Traycia was the result.

Traycia was middle-aged, about five foot seven and always wore her hair in a ponytail. She had at least a dozen tattoos covering her body and one extra large one on her thigh in the form of an angel. Traycia loved to fish. She often referred to it as the four-letter "F" word she loved to do more than anything else.

Being the child of two important people, she was protected not only by those high up in Cuban power circles but also by extremely high up in the food chain American government officials.

Traycia "Angel" Torres, nicknamed Tat, was a warm-blooded sexy American that had put together this tough group of three guys promising them twenty grand each for their time and skills. Her cut, however, was double theirs.

The three men climbed onto the fully loaded boat as Traycia fired up the two monster engines which sounded like a battalion of motorcycles. Tat-II was the name on the back of the boat which carried a pair of white & black trim Suzuki 350 DFA six-cylinder outboard motors.

The Tat-II had a range of almost 300 miles with speeds exceeding 50 knots. The boat was capable of making the round trip from the United States to Cuba in one day, and often did. According to reports compiled by the U.S. Senate Intelligence Committee, the Tat-I, *(Traycia's first boat),* was seen in the Ft. Lauderdale area a day or two after the Emerald Green explosion. The Tat-I was later found smashed against a pier in Lake Worth.

This caused conspiracy theorists to believe the boat and its owner may have played a role in the Emerald Green sinking. That gave way to even further speculation the CIA and *The Knights of Freedom* may have also played a role in that disaster.

The Caribbean waters were becoming rough as the afternoon wore on, due to the impending hurricane less than a day away.

Experienced in navigating rough waters however, Traycia steered the Tat-II on its almost thirty-minute journey from the Miramar Marina on the south side of Cuba, out into open waters of the Caribbean Sea and eventually to a hacienda just outside of Rio San Juan, within the city limits of Santiago de Cuba. This extremely powerful boat, with huge wakes coming from its stern, could be seen approaching land for miles. Cutting their engines one hundred yards from shore, they drifted up to the dock at the compound where I lived with my wife, Christine.

The sun was still a couple of hours from setting, and the horizon was full of high cirrus clouds coupled with exceptionally large white cumulus clouds surrounded by a pink and turquoise sky. It was going to be another gorgeous sunset in the Caribbean.

Except for an occasional strong gust of wind, a tropical southeastern wind was caressing the beach at the entrance of the hacienda where several open cabanas lay in the sand baking in the warm Caribbean sun. Although a hurricane warning had been issued for the entire island of Cuba, no preparations at the hacienda had been made.

I had left my beautiful hacienda earlier that morning and was in town stocking up on supplies I and my wife planned to take to our safe house a couple of hours drive north of our beautiful home.

Christine remained at the house while I went into town to make sure the staff put away anything that could become a missile when the storm did hit. Our plan was to head north to our safe house when I returned.

When the Tat-II arrived at the dock, the crew donned their ski masks and headed up to the house. Fortunately, there were no security guards on the premises. The guards had left the hacienda to be with their families and prepare for the storm.

The suave looking thin gunman named Ronaldo Jr., same as his grandfather, and who routinely did odd kill jobs for the CIA and specifically for the ***KOF***, keyed in the combination at the gate. He signaled the others to follow behind him as he proceeded up along the poolside area until reaching the hacienda. As they arrived, they crouched down and remained hidden under the cover of privacy bushes planted in front of each window.

After a short wait, Traycia could see Christine was alone in the house. She whispered to her cohorts, “I don’t think Jason Williams is in the house.” She then made a call on her cell phone to Benedict Warren, the man who hired her.

Traycia needed to know whether to abandon their plan to capture Jason Williams or to proceed and at least abduct his wife Christine. And more importantly, would they be paid the same amount for only returning with his wife and not him.

Receiving the go-ahead, the four mercenaries maneuvered their way into the house. Ronaldo grabbed Christine from behind and slammed her to the floor. His eyes met hers, and she screamed as if he were the devil getting ready to pull her down to hell.

Ronaldo started to remove her blouse and her Capri pants, but because she was wiggling so much, he just ripped them off her, exposing her silky white bra and pink frilly panties. The two taller gunmen kneeled and held her in place while Ronaldo bound her hands and feet with plastic ties.

Although no one else was in the house, this didn't stop Christine from kicking and screaming and trying to escape their control.

Ronaldo stood up and placed the bottom of his boot on her neck. "You need to stop resisting or I will put my full weight down and cause your neck to break," he said to Christine in an American voice. The threat caused her to stop.

Once he released her neck from the bottom of his boot, although restrained with her arms tied behind her back, she wiggled as far away from the men as she could and crouched in the corner of the room, thinking this might prevent what she thought was the reason they were here.

Not sure what was going on, and fearing she would be raped, she began screaming and yelling again. Christine began kicking more wildly than before as Tat kneeled to try and calm her down.

Christine's foot forcefully connected with the

jaw of Traycia and a tooth went flying across the room. It landed under the kitchen table and out of view from her enraged captor.

"You bitch!" Traycia yelled, and in a fit of rage, punched Christine in the nose, resulting in a cracking sound. Blood began to flow from Christine's broken nose, down onto the clothes that lay on the kitchen floor.

Within seconds, the two taller Cubans unwrapped a camouflage jumpsuit from their bag, cut the plastic ties from Christine's hands and feet and worked her body into what they assumed would become her outfit for the next few days.

As Christine continued to fight back, she was jolted by the electrical charge from a powerful handheld stun gun. She immediately slumped back down to the ground and became dead weight.

With darkness beginning to take over this side of the island, they quickly placed a black burlap bag over her head and carried her back down to the dock.

Traycia fired up the boat's outboard engines and were gone just as quickly as they arrived. Heading out of the bay and out into the

Caribbean Sea, they soon pulled alongside a 190-foot Trinity Motor Yacht.

This thirty-five-million-dollar sweetheart of a yacht, with its crew of thirteen, a heliport, seven cabins and every amenity the U.S. Government could buy, was waiting for the Tat-II to arrive. The yacht was out of Delaware and was called *"The Pleasure is all Mine"*.

The yacht was owned by the Central Intelligence Agency and used for many activities including entertaining its organizational department heads. It was also used for conducting initial interviews with captives to determine where they should be relocated. Another role of this yacht was for some drug smuggling activities, mostly for their own internal use. These clandestine uses were part of the daily routine of the SOC (Southern Operations Center) of the CIA and were conducted at the expense of the American taxpayer.

The four gunmen hoisted their passenger up to the yacht's lower deck and collected a briefcase from the ship's Captain, Benedict Warren, in exchange for their troubles. Having been paid, they departed back out to sea in a northwesterly direction. The yacht headed in the same direction, but at a much slower speed.

With the ship's new cargo safely secured below deck, the yacht pulled into a hidden secluded harbor, from which they could securely contact their cargo's husband once they could find him.

It was hoped Christine would be the bargaining chip in their transaction and Jason would have the opportunity to trade his life for hers. What they didn't divulge was that neither would be set free. Both would be returned to Washington once I was on board.

The CIA paid dearly for this cargo. They paid off the gambling debt of my youngest daughter, and they paid a hundred grand to the crew of the Tat-II. This brought their outlay of cash close to half a million dollars and they still didn't have the one person they came for.

Chapter 2 – A Spiders Touch

Below deck with Christine alone in an eight by eight-foot front starboard room, was Samuel “Spider” Webb, an overweight ex-Gitmo interrogator who walked with a limp due to a bite from an inmate that chewed off a chunk of his anklebone when Spider wasn’t looking. His afro style short hair and beady eyes made him scary enough, but his reputation was worse. His wrinkled face housed a 7” scar that went from his scalp line down to his left ear, which had also been partially bitten off.

Spider inherited his nickname while stationed at Gitmo. He knew how to interrogate. He was a senior interrogator for the ***KOF*** and they paid him royally for his work. He always got results and he didn’t care whether his methods were legal or not. He was as vicious as the ***KOF*** group itself.

Spider’s specialty was not to harm his captives physically in the beginning, but rather to create the fear of what he would really do to them later if they didn’t tell him what he wanted to know. He made it clear to them if they cooperated, they could go home and not be harmed. But, if they lied to him, or didn't cooperate, then they would experience him intimately, and internally. His favorite tool was a 36" bolt cutter, which mostly he used to remove a finger or two, so it could be sent to whomever's attention his bosses were trying to get. Sometimes if he felt he was being played with, or lied to, he would remove more intimate body parts instead of a finger.

His second favorite tool was an object called a "fireplace poker." He sometimes used that to pluck out an eye or two. Regardless, he always got the information he was after. It was just a matter of how long it took, and how much fun he was having.

As Christine began to moan and regain consciousness, she could feel Spider on top of her, performing a dry hump on her head. Hearing she was awake; he removed the bag from her head and ran his fingers seductively through her hair. He moaned in the joy of touching her. Without concern for any pain he might be causing her, he removed her jumpsuit and tossed it in the corner.

"Wow," Spider said out loud. "You are one hot

bitch. I can't wait to get to the end game with you," he added.

Christine pushed away from him and looked up at his dark beady eyes. Knowing she was barely clothed, she felt this is not going to end well.

"Christine Williams," Spider said to her in a slow snarly slimy voice that ran chills through her body. "We are going to get to know each other really well over the next few days. I hope it's going to be as good for you as it's going to be for me," he smirked.

"Go to hell!" Christine shouted back at her captor.

"You need to tell me where your safe house is," Spider whispered into her ear. "Yes, we know about that my dear. We just don't know where it is located. All we want to do is reunite the two of you, so we can take a little trip back to Washington. There are some folks there that want to talk with you two again."

"Fuck you!" Christine shouted as she curled her body up into a fetal position.

"Let's at least have some foreplay before

jumping into bed together," he said as he slid his hand through her hair and let it drop to her shoulder. "And remember, once I'm inside of you," he whispered, "I can either be gentle, or I can be rough. It's going to be up to you how all this ends," he said in that slow slimy tone.

Christine was in panic mode and was desperate to find out where she was. "I have to use the bathroom," she shouted at Spider. "Or do you want me to just pee here, in my panties?" she said.

"The bathroom is right over there you sweet thing, so help yourself," he said. "There's only a little porthole, so I don't think you can squeeze through that. Just don't be too long," he added.

He waited as she wiggled herself onto her knees and made her way to the bathroom. As she moved across the room, he noted how sexy she was. He couldn't stop staring at her.

"I'll get you some food, and something to sleep on while you're in the bathroom," he said as he left her alone to pee.

Christine climbed up onto the toilet and peered out the 8-inch porthole, that was the only source of light in the tiny bathroom. She could barely see the mountains as darkness began to set in, but knew she was still in Cuba, and probably just a few miles from their hacienda.

She began to cry and knew she couldn't give Jason up, just to save her own life. She wondered if she could withstand the pain that she knew was coming if she didn't tell them what they wanted to know.

She climbed down and sat on the toilet letting her bodily fluids pour from her bladder.

Within minutes, Spider returned with a mattress and a tray of food. "Here you go, darling," he said as he dropped the mattress on the floor, and then dropped the tray of food onto the mattress. "Hope you don't mind me calling you darling, darling?" he asked. "I try to develop a close relationship with all my lovers. And you know we're going to be lovers, don't you?" he asked but didn't expect an answer.

"Tonight, I'll be leaving the ship, but I will be back in the morning. That'll give you plenty of time to think about whether you're going to be cooperative or not. I'm attending a party in Cayo Perla, which is a lover's adult-only island just off the coast of Manzanillo. My helicopter awaits me," he said as he smiled at her seductively and left the room.

The ship's captain was supposed to head toward Manzanillo that evening as well, but because he wasn't sure which side of the island the hurricane was heading, either north or south, he decided to put into a safe harbor for the next few days.

Chapter 3 – Emily

Three years ago, Christine and I acquired a large and secluded piece of land about 60 miles northeast of our hacienda, and just north of the Guantanamo Naval Base. No one knew of this purchase, not even our family. It was located on the north side of the island just outside of the Alejandro de Humboldt National Park.

There, we built a two-bedroom safe house designed to withstand any attack from air, land, or sea. The safe house was outfitted with some extremely state-of-the-art electronic equipment which prevented any surreptitious outside entity from eavesdropping on their communications. We also installed the latest in video equipment with high-level scrambling capability which helped provide for private conversations. The safe house was constructed using imported special concrete block to protect from hurricanes. And now it was about to receive its first test.

The military base had evacuated all unnecessary personnel and was secured and ready for a direct hit. However, the rest of the island was on its own.

What the forecasters didn't know was whether the storm would take a southern course after hitting the eastern tip of Cuba or whether it would take a northerly course. How it hit the mountains on the eastern side of the island would dictate its new direction.

I had been gone most of the afternoon, and the sun was just beginning to set when I arrived back home at the hacienda from my shopping trip.

I parked my thirty-year-old jeep at the bottom of the circular driveway, leaving the supplies I just purchased in the back seat. I acquired this vehicle three years ago specifically because it had no GPS. No way for anyone to track me down.

I called out for Christine as I walked the short distance to the front door of the hacienda. Hearing no reply, I felt something was not right. I couldn't put my finger on it, but everything seemed too quiet to make me comfortable.

Looking around as I approached the front door, and not seeing or hearing Christine's voice, I moved my hand down to my belt and pulled out the Beretta I always carried with me. This semiautomatic 45 Caliber weapon was adopted by the United States military as their service pistol. It was sent to me by Bill McPherson as a housewarming present since I had to leave my Glock-45 in Ft. Lauderdale.

Upon entering the hacienda, the first thing I noticed was Christine didn't come to the door to greet me. I thought she might just be in the shower, but I didn't hear any water running from upstairs.

As soon as I walked into the kitchen, I knew something bad had happened. I immediately saw Christine's bloodied clothes on the kitchen floor, forcing me to bolt against the wall and chamber my Beretta, which was drawn and aiming straight ahead. "If someone is still in the house, they are soon going to be dead," I thought to myself.

"Christine," I hollered out again. "Are you okay?" There was no response, so I slowly inched my way toward the living quarters and then up the stairs to the bedrooms. As I slowly took each step, I could sense the house was empty.

I was genuinely worried now. I went back down to the kitchen and gathered up Christine's bloodied clothes. I ran outside to find the security guards and threw her clothes into the back seat of the jeep.

"They must know something," I thought. As I ran toward the beach, I pulled out my cell phone and called Christine's number. After a few rings, it went to voicemail and in her typical sexy voice, I heard her message, *"I'm not home now as I'm probably out with my honey, holding hands and skipping along the shoreline. But if you leave a message, I will return your call when time permits."*

When the beep tone came up, I hurriedly uttered the words, "Christine, call me immediately."

I became more frantic as I headed out the gate, which I found open, to my surprise. "Where are the guards?" I thought. I approached the guard building alongside the entrance to the beach, but it was empty.

I ran back up to the house, as the wind off the Caribbean Sea began to whip up. A squall line was moving in and it began to drench me with cold hard rain.

I searched the entire hacienda again and found Christine's purse and cell phone back in the hallway. As I looked around the kitchen for more clues to her whereabouts, I saw a bloody tooth under the kitchen table. I put the tooth into my pocket and continued my search.

After ten minutes, I jumped into my jeep and drove a mile in each direction on the main road that connects the hacienda with downtown.

"Fuck," I thought to myself. "Where the hell could she be?" Drenched and now exhausted, I realized she was not here. I wanted to head up to the safe house but was afraid she'd not make it on her own if I left her here. I thought about staying at the hacienda, in case she returned, but didn't like the way the waves were beginning to come ashore. Weather-wise, things were beginning to go from bad to worse.

The waves began to crash onto the beach with such force the guard shack quickly washed away, just as the jeep began its trek northward. The hacienda would be next to feel the brunt of the storm.

I drove inland toward the mountains, but my mind ran through the places Christine could be. She didn't have transportation, so if she went somewhere voluntarily, it wouldn't be far. But that didn't make sense. I knew her exit was not a planned one, as her purse and cell phone were still at the house.

That meant someone had either taken her or she had hurt herself and was seeking medical attention. My years with the Secret Service brought me to the only rational conclusion. Someone had come and taken her.

Now I knew I needed to get to the safe house. From there, I could try and take command of this situation and work to free Christine from whomever had taken her.

Two hours later, I arrived at the safe house Christine and I had built. I quickly unloaded the hurricane supplies and lit the hurricane lanterns for light. I then powered up the generators and established communication with local shortwave radio operators I knew and trusted.

I asked some of these HAM operators to contact local hospitals in the Santiago de Cuba area and to try and find out if an

American woman with Christine's description had been brought in or checked in. I also had them contact a few of the local authorities to try and get any information on her whereabouts.

All through the night, and well into the next day, I called every HAM operator I knew to find out what they were learning. Nothing showed up. There was no information available on Christine's whereabouts.

I called all the medical facilities within a forty-mile radius of Santiago de Cuba, to no avail. The more I called and got negative results, the more worried I became.

Chapter 4 – The Interrogation

Later that night, Spider returned to the 190-foot yacht unhappy that the party was canceled due to high gusty winds and a revised forecast that Hurricane Emily looked like it was going to turn a bit south once it reached Cuba's mountain range.

The Captain informed Spider they may be leaving the ship if the storm got much worse or if those in Washington called off their search for Jason Williams until the storm passed.

Spider understood that their plans might change, and he decided to venture down to see his pretty little captive. He wasn't sure he wanted to leave her behind.

Christine had not slept much during the night but instead prayed as forcefully as she could Jason would find her and rescue her from the evil she knew lay ahead. From her tears, her makeup had pretty much washed away, and her hair was a mess. She smelled from being locked in this tiny cabin all night, with no door on the bathroom to separate her from the stench of urine and solid waste.

One thing was sure, however. She knew she would never betray Jason's whereabouts. And if that meant giving in to her captor, then that's what she would do. But she didn't know if she would be strong enough to give in to him. The thought of succumbing to her interrogator nauseated her. The only other option would be to take her own life.

She was startled when Spider entered the room. He wore a giant smile as he looked at her with lust in his eyes. "Hi baby," he said with that smirky voice. "Well, it looks like you had a rough night."

She rapidly crawled backward to get away from his touch and quickly found herself up against the wall. Spider moved closer and was almost pressing himself up against her. His lips touched her ear.

Christine whined and wiggled from side to side to move away from his closeness, but to no avail.

"Where can we find your husband?" Spider said to her in a sharp terse voice. "I'm going to hurt you really bad if you don't tell me where he could be hiding."

Having had a few too many drinks caused Spider to slightly spit on her as he was talking. His saliva flew onto her face.

Christine's head was back against the wall. Her eyes were almost bulging from her head out of fear. Without thinking, she quickly raised her knee and planted it between Spider's legs, sending him to the ground. She darted around his folded-over body and ran toward the cabin door. Unfortunately, it was locked and when she turned around, Spider was standing only inches from her.

With the intensity of a sledgehammer, his closed fist squarely landed in the middle of her mouth. He hit her so hard, several of her front teeth were crushed inward.

"Don't you ever do that to me again, you bitch," he said as he grabbed her by the throat and pushed her down onto the mattress. "Where is he?" he yelled again as he shook her head and slammed it down onto the hard floor.

Spider stood up, clearly in some pain and left the room, leaving Christine to her wounds and sobbing. A few minutes later, he peeked his head back into the room, and said to her,

"All you have to do is tell me where to find Jason, and you can go home, unharmed, whole and untouched." He then closed the door to let her think about what he told her.

The winds had picked up as another squall line came through, rocking the ship violently from one side to the other. As she tried to stand up again, the rocking of the ship brought her to her knees. She could hear high winds outside, and lots of wind and water hitting the ship. Above deck, she could hear loud crashing noises and the sound of helicopter blades turning in the wind. And then unannounced, Spider returned to her room.

He had brought with him a couple of tools that caused Christine to back away quickly in fear. She began to shake violently. She was really scared, and her stomach tightened so much, she vomited all over herself.

Spider moved away as she vomited right in front of him. He smiled and said this was not very becoming of a lady. He reached into his pocket and threw her a handkerchief that looked like it had been used to wipe other forms of bodily fluids away. As the handkerchief reached her, she immediately backed away and let it drop to the floor.

"That was not very nice," he said as he kicked the vomit-stained handkerchief to the corner of the room. "Now, it's time we got a little more serious about why you're here," he said as he moved his body up against hers.

"This is the time to talk to me," he said through a half-open smile. He put his hands on both her breasts and began to squeeze harder and harder. The metal from the bolt cutter he was holding between his arm and his body pressed against one of her breasts, and she screamed at its touch.

"I'm going to use this on you if you do not cooperate," he continued. "First, I'll just start with the nipple. Then if that doesn't produce results, I'll take the whole breast. Is that what you want?" he asked as he leered into her eyes.

Christine was shaking, as she tried looking at him with a more seductive look, hoping to get him to loosen up the grip he had on her. It didn't work.

Spider put his mouth on her mouth and used his tongue to inspect the inside of her mouth. Even with the stench of vomit on her lips, he seemed to enjoy it.

"Don't bite me," he said, "or trust me, it'll be the last thing you ever do." Christine couldn't take anymore and fell to the floor as she passed out from the horror of his touch.

It was early morning when Christine awoke, and the pain she was in was almost unbearable.

Her left hand was bandaged up and wrapped in thick gauze. She tried to back away from her hand, but it just kept following her. It was more than she could take. She screamed at the top of her lungs for help. When she looked down, she saw blood on her panties and drips of blood on the floor. She crawled into the fetal position and just rocked back and forth.

The ship was also rocking violently now, and the crew had long abandoned the yacht. The Captain, Spider, all of them, were long gone.

The door to the small cabin she was in was still locked, and water was beginning to enter the room under the door. The water level was rising, and she knew she'd need to do something. "Jason, I love you," she yelled as loud as she could. "I love you so much," she said in a faint voice as she collapsed once more onto the wet floor.

Chapter 5 – Emily Passes

"Oh my God. Sunshine," I said as I peeked my head out the front door. I was awake all night worrying about where Christine might be, and if our safe house would hold up against the storm's fierceness.

I stood in the doorway, looking out for several minutes, just enjoying the warmth and the brightness the sun brought. The storm had veered just south of the Cuban island, with its northern eyewall tracking right along the southern shoreline of Cuba.

All coastal areas along the south side of the island had been devastated. All you could hear from the HAM operators was how flattened the southern part of the island had become. Cities were devastated, and marinas and harbors saw serious boat damage. Large yachts could be found a mile inland, and smaller ships were seen dangling from trees like toy boats.

I was in constant contact with local HAM operators but did not receive one positive response with regard to Christine's whereabouts. I spoke with the local authorities in Santiago de Cuba, but they weren't much help. They told me I would have to come in and file a missing person report if I wanted their help in finding my wife. They told me there would probably be hundreds of missing people they'd be looking for, so not to expect preferential treatment.

Although there were still high winds, and squall lines that drifted overhead every hour or so, the worst of the storm had passed. There was not much damage done to the safe house, and after boarding up what I could, I headed back down to the hacienda.

It took twice the normal time to get down to the southern coast, as it appeared every tree and every rock had been thrown out onto the roadway.

When I finally made it to the hacienda's driveway, I could see there was significant damage. It appeared the hacienda itself had survived the winds and storm surge, but everything else was destroyed. Our small boat was sitting in the middle of the tennis court, and the pool had popped out of the ground and was sitting sideways.

Several of the upstairs bedroom windows were gone but everything on the main floor of the hacienda looked intact. It appeared the large trees served as a protection to the downstairs area.

I ran inside and searched every room for Christine. Without hesitation, I jumped back into the jeep and headed into town in hopes of finding her there.

The police station was in the center of Santiago de Cuba, and I knew most of the officers that worked there. Upon entering however, I ran into a crowd of about thirty locals that were all looking for help in finding missing family members.

I noticed one very tall officer standing off to the side and walked over to him. The name on the officer's name tag was Hector Ruiz. He was a tall, skinny individual for a Cuban cop, with a bent nose and what is commonly referred to as a lazy eye. I wasn't sure which eye to look at as I tried to make eye contact.

"My name is Jason Williams, and I reside at the hacienda on the west side of the beach just outside of the city," I told the officer. "My wife Christine disappeared from the compound the day before the hurricane hit. Can you help me find her?"

At first, I wasn't sure if this cop understood English, so I tried to clarify my request by talking a little slower, and with a few more hand gestures. I reached into my wallet and pulled out three one-hundred-dollar bills and folded it into the cop's hand.

"Hector Ruiz at your service," the cop looked down at me and said in a low secretive voice. "Let's step outside so we can talk more," he said as he led me out the front door.

"If you have more of these," holding up the three one-hundred-dollar bills, "we'll get along just fine," Hector said as he put his arm around my shoulder. "So, tell me what this Christine looks like," he continued, "and exactly when was the last time you saw her?"

We talked for about 10 minutes, as I described Christine to Hector. As we wrapped up our conversation, I gave him my business card, with contact information, and requested he stay in touch. Hector gave me his card and told me to call him anytime I had new or updated information. I left Hector and hoped this officer would serve as a loyal partner in the search for Christine.

I continued to drive around town, which really took a hit from the storm, showing pictures of Christine to anyone who would take the time to look. No one had any information for me.

I decided it best to go back to the hacienda and begin whatever restoration efforts I could.

Chapter 6 – The Body

Hector Ruiz had tried for two hours to reach me by cell phone, without success. He made the decision to drive out to the hacienda, to check on his rich friend, and to let me know what they had found.

When he arrived, he found me passed out on the beach. I had walked for miles that night, in both directions looking for Christine. The long day had taken its toll on me and after driving down from the safe house, searching the downtown area, and walking almost twenty miles of ocean front, I had passed out from exhaustion.

Hector kneeled and began to shake me. "Jason, Jason, wake up. It's Hector from the police station," he said as I began to moan and open my eyes.

"Did you find her?" I yelled as I opened my eyes and saw who it was that was shaking me.

"How long have you been out here Jason?" Hector asked.

"Did you find her?" I yelled at Hector again, but without any response back. Hector's lazy eye was making me nauseous, so to calm down my sickening feeling, I grabbed Hector's face and tried to focus his eyes.

Hector backed away, stood up, and straightened me up enough to walk to the house where he sat me down on an outside bench. "Jason," Hector said. "You need to listen to me, and you need to hear every word I say.

"I'm told they just found a body washed up on the shore that matches the description of your missing wife. The Cuban authorities need you to come downtown to see if you can identify the body, and they want to question you to determine if you had anything to do with her death," he said.

I went into shock. I grabbed Hector by the throat and said, "What did you say? They found what on the beach?" I yelled at Hector. "A body? How do they know it was Christine's?"

Hector was pinned up against the back of the bench, as he tried to remove my hands from his throat. "No, they're not sure, so that's why they want you to come back into town, to identify the remains. The first step in this investigation is to determine if this is your missing wife," Hector responded as he removed my grip on his throat.

"Let's go," I said. "I'll follow you in my jeep. Take me to where this body is now," I demanded.

We drove to the morgue and immediately ran into a host of Cuban police blocking the entrance to where the body was being held.

Hector's boss met me at the door and cautioned me to prepare myself for the worst. He explained they found a female body washed ashore along the beach this morning, and it looked like she had been beaten, mutilated, and thrown into the sea at the height of the hurricane.

I broke down and began to sob like a baby. "Oh no, what have I done?" I said loud enough for Hector and his boss to hear.

"What do you mean, what have you done?" Hector asked in a surprised voice. "Did you kill her?"

I responded with an answer that made me

appear guilty. "This is all my fault. If I hadn't brought her down here, she'd still be alive. I am guilty," I said through my tears and grief.

Hector, seeing he could be the hero in all this, immediately pulled out his handcuffs and cuffed my hands behind my back.

His chief, being a bit wiser than the thin tall cop, stopped Hector in his tracks and ordered the cuffs removed. "Jason was in shock and did not realize what he was saying, or what was happening to him," the chief told Hector.

I pushed the chief back as I quickly rushed past him to enter the morgue door. On the table just beyond the entrance to the lab was a table and there was Christine's body, dirty, wet, and cold looking like white marble.

"Christine," I said in a soft voice. Her body was badly bruised with a broken nose, bashed in teeth and two fingers missing from her right hand.

The coroner told Jason she had been beaten and raped viciously. He admitted they had cleaned her up a little, but they just found her lying on the beach with her body clothed in only her underclothes.

He stated that once they did an autopsy, they would know more accurately what happened to her and if there's any evidence that remained after she washed ashore.

I tried to hold her in my arms, but the two officers quickly restrained me. As I wept, I could hear the Chief tell me, "We need to preserve evidence, sir. You can't be touching her, or it could implicate you in her death," he said.

"What now?" I demanded. "Do we have any idea who might have done this to her?" I yelled.

Hector looked at the Chief, expecting him to say they thought I might have done this, but the response was not what he had hoped for.

"We found wreckage of a large yacht on the same beach where your wife was found, and we're thinking she may have been on board the yacht before it sank," the chief replied. "My guess is the ship was taking safe harbor from the storm when the winds just got to be too much," he continued. "No other bodies have been found yet, so we're thinking maybe she was just left on board to drown.

"It appears the cause of death will be

drowning. The hurricane might have saved her from further abuse," the chief added. "Maybe she was lucky the hurricane hit when it did."

Chapter 7 – The Gathering

I had the damage to the hacienda sealed off and planned for a quick gathering of family members after the memorial service.

The hacienda was unbearably oppressive without Christine. I knew she was never coming back, and I questioned whether it was worth living anymore. I sat alone at the kitchen table, trying to take in some coffee before heading to the church. After a few sips of what was now cold coffee, I stood up and wiped the tears from my face. I then closed the house up and headed downtown.

I had arranged for Christine's body to be moved to Iglesias de Santa Lucia Church, a Catholic Church in the middle of Santiago de Cuba. The church had sustained mud and water damage, but it was still standing. It had only taken a couple of days to clean the place so it could serve as a location where the people of Santiago de Cuba could come and pray.

A local funeral home helped with preparing Christine's body for the service which would be conducted by the priest that remarried Christine and me shortly after we arrived in Cuba.

Justin, Tonya, and Teresa had flown in that morning and were sitting in the first row, just in front of the closed casket I had arranged. This was an emotional disaster for Justin, now twenty, as he and his mother were awfully close. Her body was too savagely beaten to display in open casket. All the makeup in the world wouldn't hide what they did to her face and body.

Sitting beside them was my sister Charlene and her current partner Elisabeth, both consoling Justin as best they could. They flew in the night before and were staying at the hacienda with me.

Justin, our son and the youngest of our children, was blurry eyed with tears as he held the hands of his two sisters, Tonya and Teresa. As expected, both girls were completely grief-stricken and upset. They were in desperate need of their younger brother's support and companionship.

Sitting in the last row behind those in attendance, surrounded by ten large white columns, five on each side of the church, was Dylan Rains. He was sitting beside Anthony Esposito who made the journey down to Cuba from Las Vegas, even though he was just a year or so shy of eighty.

I had not seen Dylan in over two years. Dylan had left the island a couple of years ago, breaking up with his then-girlfriend, Serena Diaz. Their arrangement didn't last long due to the kind of life Dylan lived. He was always on the run and had decided to leave the Cuban island in a hurry once discovering the United States was again the topic of terrorist conversation on the dark web.

Dylan had apparently uncovered the existence of an agreement between Assam Bashula, the President of Syria, and someone from inside *The Knights of Freedom*, that could become the beginning of the end for the United States.

All he could tell was it had something to do with chemical weapons and drones. This was something he needed to learn more about and couldn't from within Cuba and its limited internet capabilities.

Dylan had let himself go, appearance-wise, and now looked like a homeless bum. His clothes were musty looking, and his hair was long and unruly and at least ten to fifteen inches long. It stood straight up like an Afro from the sixties that went wild. His beard was scraggly, and he smelled like he hadn't bathed in years.

Anthony was responsible for liquidating my American assets, which ended up being several million dollars. He would sometimes send down tens of thousands of dollars a month, in cash, hidden in shoe boxes addressed to Christine. He was dressed in a fine suit, Italian shoes and a tie that probably cost $500 or more.

****

The Reverend Maria DeAngelis began the service with a greeting to all those in attendance. She was young and had only been with the church five or six years. Christine and I were the first wedding she performed in Cuba and had befriended us both when we first arrived.

She then continued with a prayer of assurance, followed immediately with the singing of a hymn which was meant to celebrate the life of this beautiful young and vibrant woman. The Reverend's thirty-minute tribute ended with a reading of the scripture.

Justin was the first to come forward and speak about his mother. His lower lip quivered as he told of the years she alone raised him. "She gave up everything to get me into college," Justin said as he teared up. "And she never stopped being there for me," he told the congregation.

After a few minutes, Tonya and Teresa joined him alongside the casket. Tonya pulled out a couple of 3x5 index cards and used them to tell a few jokes about her mom. Teresa held Tonya's hand, and when there was a small break in Tonya's quips, Teresa jumped in and said how much she loved her mom.

Then Teresa lost control and began a tirade about hating her father. "We're all going to miss her," Teresa said as her voice began to rise. "Her death is on your hands," she yelled as she pointed to me. "I hate you for killing our mother," Teresa continued. "If you hadn't put everything else ahead of our family, forcing the two of you to flee the country, she would still be alive," she yelled as she broke down and sobbed uncontrollably.

The church's organ began to play, and recorded voices of a choir could be heard singing in the background:

Amazing grace! How sweet the sound,
That saved a wretch like me!
I once was lost, but now am found.
Was blind, but now I see.

This was followed by the Reverend leading those in attendance with a familiar hymn.

After the hymn, friends and family listened to reflections by Reverend DeAngelis, who knew Christine well. The Reverend had provided her with spiritual guidance and support during the three years she was in Cuba.

She told everyone that Christine and I visited her church every Sunday and were always supportive of the needs of the community and the church. The Reverend praised us for giving money and much of our own time to support causes she needed help with. I moaned out loud in sorrow and pain, as I listened to the words of the Reverend.

"No love has ever been greater than the love Christine and Jason shared over the years," the Reverend began. “Christine would do anything for the man she so adored, and he would do anything for her,” she continued. “Jason,” she quoted, “would say to her every night before going to bed, how lucky he was. That she made him a king by forgiving him for the years he ignored his family and gave all to the country he thought he loved more. She was his life now, and all that mattered to him, he would tell her.

“It was clear to anyone who knew them that what he said about her was true. That she was the result of a lifelong search for the girl of his dreams. He was to her and she was to him,” the Reverend continued as tears and wet eyes prevailed throughout the attendance.

I sat alongside the closed casket and couldn’t hold back the tears. I kept one hand on the casket and in the other hand, held the tribute card that was provided to those attending the memorial service. My focus was just not there.

The card read:

Don’t remember me with sadness,
Don’t remember me with tears,
Remember all the laughter,

We've shared throughout the years.
Now I am content
That my life it was worthwhile,
Knowing that as I passed along the way
I made somebody smile.
When you are walking down the street
And you've got me on your mind,
I'm walking in your footsteps
Only half a step behind.
So please don't be unhappy
Just because I'm out of sight,
Remember that I'm with you
Each morning, noon and night.

Jesus said, "I am the resurrection and the life. Those who believe in me, even though they die, will live." – John 11:25

I tried four or five times to read the poem on the card but after starting over numerous times, I put it down and held my head in my hands as I began to cry.

Trying to regain my composure, I stood and kissed the coffin that would soon be transported back to Christine's hometown of Middlebury, Vermont. We had made pre-need plans for Christine to be buried at Hope Cemetery, which was about an hour-and-a-half southeast of Burlington, Vermont. That's where the few recovered remains of her parents, who died in the north tower of the World Trade Center on September 11, 2001, are located, and she wanted to be buried alongside their graves.

The Reverend asked if anyone else would like to come forward and share a few words, however, no one did.

At the end of the service, the procession stood and formed a line that would allow them to pass by Christine's casket and offer whatever prayers they could. As each person who attended the service came up to me, and offered solace and comfort, my rage began to fester.

As those from my past proceeded by me, standing alongside her beaten and battered body, I looked at them with daggered and piercing eyes. After the last person paying their respects passed by me, I kneeled, putting my hands over top of the casket, and said, "Goodbye my darling. I love you."

Although everyone at the church was loved by both of us, I knew someone had to pay for her death and the cruelty that was imparted on her.

And I knew the United States Government

had helped *The Knights of Freedom* locate our whereabouts. And I knew they participated in the abduction of my wife. They would suffer my revenge, I thought to myself.

The two hundred attendees of the memorial service proceeded past the coffin. They then exited the church and gathered in the beautiful courtyard, where grieving was the task at hand. After the funeral, the entire family returned to the hacienda to reflect on what had happened and where would they go from here.

I had arranged for a small home memorial service just for the immediate family. Food and drinks were available, as was a private video and slideshow of many of Christine's most favorite activities. Each family member was in the slideshow, and it showed Christine during the happy moments of her life.

My brother Douglas, currently the Vice President of the United States, pulled me into the kitchen and casually asked if I knew who was responsible for Christine's death.

"I know who is responsible," I said with rage in my heart, and revenge in my voice. "And you know as well. It was the damn *Knights of*

Freedom. And particularly Granger Adams," I responded. "I don't know how he found me," I shouted, "but he will pay for what he did."

"Calm down brother," Douglas said in a soft consoling voice. "We'll take care of those that betrayed you and they'll pay dearly," Douglas added. "Let's just try to bring some good out of this if we can," Douglas said as his thoughts returned to images of Christine. "You know she would have wanted something good to come from her passing," he continued.

"Let's meet later to put a plan in motion to go up against the ***KOF***," Douglas said as he put his arm around me and brought me close to him for a hug. We held each other for several minutes, and I thanked Douglas for his support, and for being there in my time of need.

As I patted my brother on the back, my daughter Tonya walked into the kitchen. "There you are," Tonya said as she found the two brothers hugging.

Unable to hold back her own tears, she thrust herself forward and into the arms of the both of us.

Out on the veranda, Teresa was downing her

third straight Elijah Craig bourbon on the rocks and was not amused by the home movies being shown in the other room. Douglas and I saw her out on the balcony and walked out there to speak with her.

"This is your fault," she shouted out to me. "If you had not been so damn focused on saving the world, our mother would still be alive today," she ranted. "I hate you, and I hate all you stand for," she shouted again with bitterness in her voice. "You never cared a damn about any of us, and this is the result of your doing," she yelled as she threw her drink at me and stormed off the balcony.

Douglas put his drink down and went after her, ending up outside by the pool which was still sticking out of the ground.

"Teresa," he said as he reached her sobbing by the pool's cabana. "It's okay baby," he said. "This is hard on all of us. Please try to understand your father loved your Mom very much and he did everything he did for you and for her," he said in a soft voice.

"That's pure bullshit," she turned and said to Douglas. "You know it and I know it. My Dad does not now, nor did he ever give a fuck about any of us."

She looked into Douglas's eyes and demanded he acknowledge what everyone already knew. That her Dad is a phony, and he killed her mom. She left him years ago because of his lifestyle and she thought he changed so she came back to him.

"Why did he have to leave the United States, and take her away from us, her children?" she said with her face up against Douglas's face.

"Well, I'll tell you why," she continued not giving Douglas a chance to answer. "So, he could be in control of her, and prevent her from enjoying her family.

"Well, I'll be no part of this charade," Teresa shouted as she pulled away and headed down toward the driveway. "I've called a cab, and I'm leaving this place and this country. I'm not staying here another moment. I hate him, and I hate everyone that supports what he does. I'm glad I told them where to find him," she mumbled as she stormed away, hoping no one heard her uncontrolled outburst.

Douglas thought about going after her but realized there was nothing he would be able to say that would calm Teresa down. "Better she gets it out of her system now," he thought to himself.

I walked over to Douglas, who was now back in the kitchen, and put my arm around his shoulder. "What was all that about?" I asked in a low voice.

"What was what all about?" Douglas responded, thinking he needed a drink as well, but didn't dare walk away from me in my current state of mind.

"You know, out by the pool that's half sticking out of the ground, with Teresa," I said.

"Oh, she was just blowing off steam. She's pretty pissed at you, thinking this is all your fault," he replied, choosing not to bring up her final comment about telling them where we could be found.

"Well, it is," I answered back. "If I hadn't been so pig-headed, and just handled all that ***KOF*** stuff privately, this wouldn't be our situation now," I said in disgust.

"Don't blame yourself," Douglas responded. "It is what it is, and you had to do what you had to do."

“I know who is responsible for Christine’s abduction and torture,” I offered. I couldn’t say the word death. “But I don’t know the name of the individual that did this to my wife,” I added.

“Will you help me bring them down?” I begged my brother. “We’re having a meeting tonight, once all the guests leave, to put together a plan that will retaliate for the abduction and torture of my wife. If they thought I did damage before, wait until they see who I plan to take down now. Are you in?” I asked.

“Yes, I am,” Douglas responded. “Wouldn’t miss it for the world. But we also must deal with Teresa’s anger. She could become a problem for you down the road,” he added.

“Yep, it’ll all be on the table. We can discuss this all tonight. Dylan Rains and Anthony will also be attending our strategy meeting, so we can assess who is in and who is not,” I added.

Chapter 8 – The Plan

It was around 5:00 P.M. when Tonya called a cab and headed to the airport, leaving some incredibly angry and determined folks to plot retaliation for what happened to Christine.

Dylan, Anthony, Douglas, and Justin were already at the bar when I arrived. Bourbon and vodka were flowing freely.

"I am extremely touched and want to personally thank the four of you for being here with me at this very sad moment in my life," I said. "Christine was my very heartbeat, and the scum bags that did this to her must pay. They must pay dearly," I repeated.

"I will pluck the eyes out of the bastard that did this to Christine. This didn't need to happen to her," I said as my anger began to fester. "I will avenge her death," I said again very loud and very slowly.

I started to pour myself a bourbon and water, but instead threw the bottle of Jack Daniels against the mirror behind the bar. Glass shattered everywhere, and a few pieces found their way onto the top of the bar. Dylan and Anthony ducked out of the way of the flying bottle, but Douglas and Justin caught some of the glass in their drinks.

"I'm sorry guys," I said as I broke down again. "Please, forgive me."

Anthony and Dylan reached out to me, and both put their arms around me. "Christ," I said as I recomposed myself. "I'm so sorry," I said as I bit my lower lip which was beginning to quiver.

"I'm okay, just pissed," I said as I pulled out another bottle of Jack and headed over to one of the two leather couches in the middle of the room.

Justin and Douglas found new glasses and refilled their drinks. They joined me on the couch. Anthony and Dylan sat across from us.

"Dylan my friend," I said as I looked Dylan up and down. "You smell. You need to go upstairs and take a shower and groom all that hair. I love you, man," I said, "but you're smelling up the place.

"I plan to avenge her death," I said, but began

to quiver as I used the "D" word. "This will not be easy," I continued, "and the result will have disastrous consequences. *The Knights of Freedom* are deeply entrenched into our government, and the entire course of history will be changed by what we are about to do.

"As you know, we're dealing with some immensely powerful people, many of whom are in our country's highest level of government. You all know their plans, and you know what they're capable of if they find out you're involved with me in a plan to take them down. I don't want to understate the danger involved," I added.

"Look what they did to Christine. To find out where my safe house was, they cut off two of Christine's fingers, they tattooed *(or should I say branded),* her body with the letters ***KOF***, they raped her and used the handle of some type of tool to physically molest her. And they bashed her face in," I said as I began to choke up.

"God only knows the pain she suffered during all this. Her drowning probably saved her from further suffering. My poor baby," I sobbed. "This is all my fault."

Dylan Rains was quite distraught seeing his good friend in such pain. He rubbed my shoulder, as he leaned over the coffee table between the two couches and took charge.

"Listen," Dylan began, "we all know what the eventual goal of the ***KOF*** is. What we need is a multi-phased approach that will initially let them continue to think no one can defeat them or their goal. We want them to think no one here is leading any kind of retaliation effort to overthrow them. We want them to think they scared Jason Williams and his team to death, and into remission," he continued. "If we can cause them to lower their defenses, then we'll have a chance to infiltrate and bring them down from within.

"The first phase should be to let them capture you," he said looking directly at me. "That way, they'll think they're safe and will lower their defenses altogether."

I looked up and said, "That's not a good idea my friend. If they capture me, you'll all be sitting around the table mourning me, like we're mourning Christine.

"But," I continued, "if they do capture me, you guys will need to put together a rescue plan that keeps them from knowing I've been rescued." I looked at Dylan and said, "Please put on your 'To Do List' how you're going to do that," I said with a laugh.

Ignoring my humor, Anthony interrupted, "Once they've got you, we need to figure out a way to infiltrate their organization."

"You got it," Dylan responded. "The ***KOF*** is nothing but a large whale, with high government officials guiding its direction. Because of its size, it doesn't change directions quickly. I think its size can be used against it and eventually lead to its downfall. We just need to somehow get one of our people into the head of this giant, so we can begin to alter its direction and lead it out to sea where it will eventually drown," he responded.

"Well, how the hell do we do that?" Justin asked.

"Easy," said Douglas. "By putting one of us deep inside that organization. And I can tell you right now who that one person should be. None of you will ever be welcomed back into the White House again, well, maybe Justin since he's still a kid and wouldn't be suspected of anything. So, it's got to be me," Douglas said as he downed his shot of bourbon.

"I know their plan better than anyone here," Douglas continued. "Basically, they are quickly moving to approve the joint resolution just passed by Congress and begin submitting it and the amendments to the States for ratification. Once ratified, this will allow the existing POTUS to approve further amendments to the Constitution without ratification by the States."

"And their first order of business," I said, "will be to alter the Constitution to allow states to secede quickly, easily, and legally."

"Once that is done," Dylan jumped back into the conversation, "Granger Adams will have his eleven southern states secede and form a new country. At that point, Bill McPherson will probably appoint Granger Adams the first president of the United Southern States of America. They both will go down in history forever."

"Yes, then I agree," said Justin. "You're already part of their team, so you would be the right person to lead the attack. However, we're also going to need another front that attacks from the legal side. Once we implement any kind of take-down effort, the courts will get involved, and it might even go to the Supreme Court. We'll need to be ready with that attack as well," he suggested. "I can lead that effort," Justin added.

"This is like the old days," Anthony said as he tossed his hat into the ring. "I may be getting old, but I still have some influence with the mob. We're going to need inside information on these guys and I can get blackmail material on all of them, easily. The guys I deal with have got lots of beautiful babes that can suck every piece of information out of these guys you'll ever need -- literally," he laughed. "I can't wait to start up old operations again. I'll gather my mob friends back together once I return to Vegas.

"We're also going to need a place to bring you, near Washington D.C., once we to rescue you," Anthony continued. I'll have our guys checkout farmhouse's in the Virginia hills somewhere," he said.

I couldn't believe how much my loyal friends were willing to give, to avenge what happened to my beloved wife. I loved what I was hearing and raised my glass for a toast. The rest of the gang did the same. “To Christine,” we all said in unison.

Chapter 9 – Lock & Load

It was dark when I returned from taking Douglas to the airport and dealing with Christine's casket which the funeral home was sending up to Vermont. My head was pounding as I parked the jeep at the bottom of the driveway and slowly walked back up to the hacienda. I was exhausted, both physically and mentally.

I needed a drink, but before doing anything of the sort, I pulled out my cell phone and looked up the telephone number of Sergei Petrov, a local Russian gun dealer who ran a chain of large gun emporiums in the United States.

For the last few years, Sergei has lived in Santiago de Cuba. He came to Cuba in the early 60's, along with the missiles the Russians sent here. Although he does a great business in the United States, the U.S. will not allow him residence there. Living here, he was only an hour away from his newest gun range on South Beach, just a few minutes south of Miami.

I had frequented Sergei's South Beach giant indoor emporium several times just to keep my marksmanship skills fine-tuned. Sergei created a new concept in gun ranges. It was more of a country club atmosphere, with restaurants, retail counters and everything a gun owner would want to purchase. It was a candy store for gun owners.

I met Sergei on my first visit to his South Beach location, and we became fast friends. Sergei is an older fellow, but still, the ladies' man who talks with a Russian accent and a slight slur he developed after spending a year in Boston, Massachusetts.

Sergei was born and raised in Kosh-Agach, Altay, Russia. This is an area that's part of the Siberian Federal District, which is located on the southern border of Russia, between Kazakhstan and Mongolia. The town he lived in was not far from the Chinese border. Because of where he comes from, he was given the nickname "Koshi."

Koshi once told me, "I love *two-thousand-dollar-a-night hookers, but in Cuba, it only cost two-hundred-dollars a night.*" He once further joked, "*in Thailand, it's only two-dollars a night*".

I pressed the call button on my cell phone.

"Hello," Sergei answered in a soft but cautious voice.

"Koshi, it's me, Jason Williams. We met several times in South Beach. Christine and I attended your 70th birthday party downtown at the Hotel Punta Gorda earlier this year as guests of the mayor. I hope I'm not catching you at a bad time?" I asked.

"Yes, how are you?" Sergei responded back. "No, not at all," he continued. "I'm so sorry to hear about Christine. If there is anything I can do for you, please don't hesitate to ask," he continued.

"Well, there is something you can do for me Koshi," I responded with a little more authority. "I'd like to meet with you as soon as possible, maybe tomorrow, if that's okay? I am looking to purchase a few guns and some ammo, and I'm going to need it transported to your emporium just outside Washington D.C., in Alexandria, Virginia. Can you do this for me?" I asked.

"No problem my friend," Sergei said. "Whatever you need, I'll take care of it for you. I am available tomorrow if you would like. Did you have a specific place you'd like to meet?" he asked.

"How about downtown at the Hotel Punta Gorda, say around noon?" I replied.

"Perfect," Sergei responded. "And what specifically were you interested in acquiring?" Sergei asked.

"I'm looking to acquire a few dozen weapons," I said. "Mostly, I'd like some high-powered semi-automatic and fully automatic rifles, with scopes. And I could use a few flamethrowers and a few Rocket Propelled Grenade Launchers (RPG)," I added. "If you can fix me up, I'll pay in cash," I told Sergei.

"I can get you whatever you need Jason, and it will be half price for you. I just need to cover my costs," he continued. "You and your wife were a blessing to our city, and we are forever indebted to you. I will look forward to seeing you tomorrow and to repay you for all the good things you and Christine did," he replied as we ended our conversation.

The next day at exactly noon, I pulled up in front of the Hotel Punta Gorda in downtown

Santiago de Cuba. Standing out front was my friend Koshi. "Jason," Sergei said as he extended his hand, meeting my hand halfway.

I parked the car and we walked to a couch in the lobby that was semi-private and made ourselves comfortable.

"There are three specific rifles I'm seriously interested in," I began. "The first is the AK-47's for its reliability. The second is the AR-15's and the third is the M27's. Can you get these for me?" I asked.

"The first two should be no problem," Koshi responded. "However, the M27 Infantry Automatic Rifle, although made in the United States, is tightly controlled by your government. It is used by your Marines and its availability outside the government is limited."

"But" he said, "I have friends, so I may be able to get you a few of them. But only a few," he smiled at me and winked. "What are you going to use these weapons for?" Koshi asked.

"There is a need to be able to take down, from a long distance, individuals that have committed treason against my country," I said. "So, hopefully, a single shot will be enough to terminate them, but if not, I'll need to be able to get off additional quick shots," I added.

"What if I can get you a weapon that will only need one shot, and one that you can't miss with?" Koshi whispered softly to me. "What if it were a laser beam that you focused on your target, pulled the trigger, and bam, they're dead?" Koshi continued.

"No matter what part of the body you hit, they would die from the damage caused by the laser's heat. Would you be interested in something like that?" he asked.

I nodded my interest, so Koshi continued. "A few years ago, the Chinese developed a military grade weapon known as the "Zeeker" ZKZM-500. They've improved this weapon to the point where it's now lightweight, uses mini lithium batteries, and can hit a target over a thousand yards away. Their new ZKZM-700A can reportedly cause sudden death by burning the human skin beyond human tolerance. The weapon is silent, and there is no gunshot sound. And the beam is invisible, lending itself to covert military operations. The laser beam can even pass through glass to its eventual target," Koshi said. "It also now has the ability to dial back the strength of the beam, so if you only want to wound your target, you could fire a less powerful beam," Koshi added.

"Wow, that sounds perfect," I told Koshi. "I like that much better. Lighter weight, no heavy ammo to lug around, and deadly," I added.

"I can get my hands on a dozen or so of these if you'd like. They're a little pricey, around $2,500 each at half price, but they'll do the job, and no one will be the wiser about what happened."

We shook hands on the deal, and Koshi said he would arrange to store the weapons at his emporium just outside Washington D.C. and he could deliver them where and when I needed.

"Perfect," I said. "I will have someone contact you soon with an eventual address as to where these need to be delivered, and enough lead time so you can get them there without getting yourself in trouble. I don't need them right away. Take a month if you need it," I told Koshi.

"Yes, this may take a little doing," Koshi told me. "I might have to make a couple of trips there to hide what you're asking for. The ATF has been watching me closely in case I sell arms to groups they feel shouldn't have them," he said.

"Be careful," I told him. "There is a lot of change coming to Washington D.C. and the country, and gun control could really tighten up."

"Yes, I know," said Koshi. "They're already tightening the screws on my gun emporiums. I may have to close a couple of my stores in the northeast area. They love my operation down south, but it's getting difficult to expand outside of that area."

I told Koshi I needed a few days to gather up the cash and I would call him by the end of the week to settle. We shook hands to seal our agreement.

Being somewhat careful, we departed the hotel about 15 minutes apart. Later, Koshi texted me with an amount to bring the next day. The half-priced cost would be $25,000.

Before leaving town, I made one final stop at the local Verizon store, which had been in Cuba since the Embassies were reopened in 2015. *(Cuba's national phone company is ETECSA, and they are responsible for cell phone service for most of the Caribbean.)*

There, I purchased a dozen burner phones. The store, like most of the town, had reopened for business after the hurricane but was operating on limited hours.

I headed back to the safe house to await the second phase of our plan.

Chapter 10 – The Ship

Once at the safe house, I began to think about what my next step would be.

Pulling myself up from the recliner, I went to the safe and removed the $25,000 in cash, plus a $3,000 bonus, that would be needed to settle with Koshi.

I knew today would be the first day in my new role to avenge my wife's death. I shaved all hair from my head and trimmed my week-old beard to just a goatee and a mustache. I looked more Cuban than some of the local Cubans themselves.

After cleaning up and putting on some camouflage army pants and matching shirt, I called Hector Ruiz, the Santiago de Cuba Police officer I befriended. I needed to talk with him about the ship's wreckage they found on the same beach where Christine's body had washed ashore.

"This is Hector Ruiz," the voice on the other end of the phone said in a cheery tone. "How can I help you?" he asked.

"Hector, it's me, Jason Williams. Do you have a minute to chat with me? I need to ask you about what had washed up on the shoreline when you found my wife's body," I said.

"Ah, yes," he replied. "We can get together if you'd like. Where are you now Jason?" Hector asked.

"I'm home," I responded, knowing I was lying to protect my whereabouts, "but we can do this over the phone if you wouldn't mind," I added. "I just have a few questions for you if you have a moment."

"What can I do for you?" Hector asked hesitantly, hoping he could come out and meet with me. I sensed he felt I was involved in her death and he wanted nothing more than to pin this on me and become the hero of Santiago de Cuba.

"Well," I began. "I'd like to know if you've been able to uncover any further information about the ship wreckage that was also found near my wife's body. Were you able to identify the name of the ship or its owner? Were there any other bodies found in the same area? Is there any new information you can share with me that would help to solve who did this to my wife?"

"Well, yes we did find two more bodies a mile down that beach. They looked like deckhands of some type. We also found the stern of the ship with a partial name on it," Hector said. "It looks like the ship's name had the word *'Pleasure'* in it. We are tracking down all ships that came through Cuba's ports up to a week prior to the storm. Should I let you know when we get a hit on the name?" Hector asked.

"I may be hard to reach over the next few weeks, so if it's okay with you, I'll just check in with you every few days or so," I said.

"Sure," Hector responded.

"And I may be in town later next week, so if it's okay with you, we could maybe get together for lunch and catch up. How's that sound?" I asked.

"Yes, that would be fine. Oh, by the way, I thought you should know there was a new development uncovered at the autopsy. It appears your wife was raped by some type of hand tool," he said. "Fifteen cut marks were found inside her vaginal area. I'd say whoever did this was a real pervert," he added. "The official cause of death from the coroner, however, is still drowning," Hector added.

"Thanks for the information Hector," I said as I hung up the phone. "What a fucking idiot," I thought.

Turning to my laptop, and using satellite wi-fi, I did a search on pleasure yachts of at least 140' with the name *"Pleasure"* as part of the ship's registered name, but came up with no results. "So," I thought, "there is no ship of that size registered to any of the Caribbean islands with the word *'Pleasure'* in it. Then it could be a United States registered vessel, possibly registered on the east coast of the mainland since it was in the Caribbean."

Signing off the Secret Service web search I still had access, I turned to the dark web and found a ship called *'The Pleasure is all Mine'*, registered out of Delaware, to the Altec Cement Company.

I knew the Altec Cement Company was a CIA shell corporation used to hide the flow of money in and out of the United States for clandestine purposes. On a roll, I decided to continue my search on the dark web for information about *The Knights of Freedom*.

It did not take but a second for hundreds of hits to be listed referencing this group. There were links to known members of this group, and to the group's Charter. Just about everything I wanted to know about this group was there. I tagged those sites I wanted to revisit and continued searching for information.

I decided it was time to get Dylan Rains caught up on the latest developments. This was getting too deep for me to handle by myself, and I had to be sure the names I was beginning to compile were the ones involved in Christine's death. It was hard getting information through the access that was available in Cuba.

I put a call into Dylan reaching his voicemail. As the beep sounded, I said, "Dylan, call me tonight at 7:00 P.M. my time, so we can talk. I have new information for you."

I then hung up the phone and knew since I was calling from the safe house, Dylan would recognize the phone number and should call back tonight.

While waiting for a call back from Dylan, I reviewed the plan my team put together:

- The initial effort of the plan called for me to setup delivery of the weapons my freedom fighters would need to engage *The Knights of Freedom*.

- The second step was to get myself abducted by the CIA, giving the ***KOF*** a reason to let down their guard.

To accomplish this second step, I planned to contact an old acquaintance I knew from a few years back and ask him to smuggle me back into the United States. I knew this individual would contact the CIA and give me up, to clear the way for bringing girls and drugs illegally into the country. I knew I could count on my old friend Hap, to sell me out.

Once captured, I knew I would have to remain in captivity for up to six months. The KOF had to feel comfortable knowing they had captured the only person who could stop them from their goal of creating a new country within the United States of America. I knew I would need to remain in custody long enough for my team to identify every person that was involved in Christine's abduction and death. Their tasks were:

- **Dylan,** who was an expert with a software product known only to law enforcement called "Geofeedia," would use this immensely powerful social media snooping program to locate each person on the list. Dylan would use "Geofeedia" to scan all known social media sites for an individual. This then would uncover the individual's current location based on IP addresses and the location of those participating in the social media event.

- **Douglas** would be channeling all information to Dylan about the group's nationwide political, corporate, and financial structure. This was necessary to physically bring down the *Knights of Freedom* and equally as important, of reversing the destruction to the United States of America.

- **Anthony** would be providing all the necessary funding to execute this plan. The resources of Anthony's Bellagio Hotel were bountiful and unending, and he was making it available to me to use as I saw fit.

- **Justin** would be directing all legal efforts to ensure the Supreme Court of the United

States was kept current of our status. They, in the end, would have to rule on the legality of those states seceding from the United States and on the legality of the Constitutional amendments. And more importantly, on the legality of undoing what the ***KOF*** puts in place during its reign of power.

- **Dylan's main military team,** the United-Six, had the responsibility of locating and then breaking me out of confinement. They would also be responsible for the termination of those involved in Christine's death and of disposing of their bodies as well.

Chapter 11 – His Name was Spider Webb

"Hello Dylan," I said answering the phone call that came exactly at 7:00 P.M. "You are punctual as usual."

"Yes, I am," he responded. "You'll be glad to know that I've just spent the last few days gathering my old gang together and bringing them up to speed on our plan to take down the ***KOF***."

"Dylan," I interrupted. "I need to bring you up to date on a few things. This will help you identify who was involved in Christine's death."

"I'm listening," Dylan responded.

"I've discovered that the ship she was being held on belonged to the CIA. Not directly, but through one of their shell corporations. The name of the ship was *The Pleasure is all Mine,* and I was able to confirm that Granger Adams spent a lot of time on board this ship during the past year. He and his buddies at the CIA are behind all this.

"There are a couple of other names I've uncovered, that have also cruised the Caribbean on board this vessel. I need you to check them out and find out if they, in fact, were involved in Christine's abduction.

"The first is Benedict Warren, who I understand was the Captain of this ship during the time of Christine's abduction. There is also a lead interrogator that was used heavily in Gitmo and is now used exclusively by the ***KOF***. He is known by the nickname of Spider Webb. He is a pervert with a sick mind and a compulsion to harm those he is paid to interrogate," I said. "He used to work for the CIA, but now is paid by *The Knights of Freedom*.

"I also found out," I continued, "he was in this area during the time Christine was killed. I'm told he was to attend a private party on one of the local islands the day before the hurricane hit. Considering how we found Christine, I think he's the man I really want to get to meet personally," I said without interruption.

"No problem boss," Dylan responded. "I'll get right on it."

"Also," I interrupted, "see if you can get a handle on Christine's kidnappers. I found a tooth in the kitchen where they abducted her, and it might be from one of her captors. Maybe you can do something with DNA," I added. "How do you want me to get it to you?"

"Send it to my P.O. box," Dylan responded. "You still know the number?" he asked me.

"Yep, I got it on my phone."

"Good, then mail it there. By the way," Dylan said, "if it makes you feel more comfortable, we are ready to extract you from Gitmo when the time comes. We will be monitoring the dark web to obtain your exact location once they capture you. Try and give us as much time as possible, and once we have everything in place, we'll come rescue you. Just know this may not happen overnight. It could take several weeks to get you out when the time is right. So just sit tight and know we will come for you my friend," Dylan said.

Chapter 12 – Enter Carlos

It was late evening when I drove my jeep back down to the hacienda. Most of the roads were still blocked, and this was backwoods country and very mountainous, so I knew there would be a lot of evidence a hurricane had just passed through a few days ago.

Due to the debris, it took almost three hours to reach the hacienda. The guard shack was still nothing but a pile of rubble, and the pool was going to take major work to repair.

As I walked down to what remained of the guard shack, I noticed some wood movement under the rubble. I then saw a gun attached to an arm rise from under the pile of crumbled building. The gun was aimed at me.

I moved to the side and grabbed a 2x4, which I used to smack the gun from the arm that was holding it. “Get out of there,” I hollered, “or I’ll kill you where you lie,” I continued.

Within a moment, a grungy, stubble-haired, long-bearded, tall, ugly man stood up and tried climbing out from the debris. As he stumbled trying to get up, I demanded he put his hands behind his head and drop to his knees. The man never did look to see if I was pointing a gun at him, which I was not since I didn't have one in my possession. It was in the glove compartment of my jeep.

"Who are you?" I yelled at the deranged looking fellow.

"My name is Carlos," the shabby-looking man exclaimed. "I was just looking for a place to sleep, and I saw no one was home here," he said. "Who are you?" the man asked of me.

"I'll ask the questions here," I yelled back at him. "Where did you come from?" was the question tossed back to Carlos who looked like he hadn't slept in several days.

"I'm homeless sir, and I was in town, but everything there is being cleaned up and restored, so I had to leave Santiago de Cuba," he replied

"Okay then, put your hands down. If you're willing to work and help clean up this place, I'll let you stay at the hacienda. There's probably even a spare bedroom there for you.

You're welcome to bed down there if you'd like," I told Carlos. "Come on, I'll let you in," I said as we both walked up the hill.

I kept an eye on Carlos, as I wasn't sure how safe I would be with him in the house. As we approached the house, I slipped on a pile of rubble, but Carlos caught me and prevented me from getting hurt. This did make me feel a little better about my new-found friend.

The hacienda was clean downstairs and there wasn't much work that was needed there. That was downstairs. Upstairs was another matter. Since water had made its way into the upstairs bedrooms and bathrooms, both of us would have to sleep downstairs. I had brought food from the safe house, so I made sandwiches for me and Carlos.

"I'll be leaving here in the morning," I explained to Carlos, "so I'd like you to begin with the upstairs. The windows need to be boarded up, and the mess from all the wind and water needs to be addressed. That'll be your first work assignment."

"Gotcha," Carlos said. "You can count on me."

Before retiring for the evening, I put a call

into Koshi and informed him I was ready to settle on his tab. We agreed to meet at the same location as before.

The next morning, with a suitcase full of cash I brought down from the safe house to pay Koshi, I headed downtown.

While on the drive downtown, I made a call to Anthony Esposito using one of the burner phones. Anthony answered his cell phone almost immediately, not knowing who was calling and simply said, “Can I help you.”

I quickly responded to Anthony, saying “It’s me, Jason.”

“Where are you?” Anthony asked.

“I’m still at the hacienda but will be getting ready to implement the next phase of our plan within the next day or two. I have a few arrangements to iron out yet, but I should be able to get things going by then,” I said. “I need to know if you and Justin were able to acquire a farmhouse in Leesburg yet?” I asked.

“Yes,” responded Anthony. “I acquired two. Just a few hundred yards apart from each other. You never know when we may need a backup place to hide," he added. "I'll send you the address of the main house as soon as I can," he continued.

"No, don't do that. I can't tell my captors something I don't know," I responded. "Dylan and I discussed the details of my escape plan yesterday, so you won't hear from us again until we're back in the United States," I stated and then terminated the call.

I arrived at the Punta Gorda Hotel a few minutes before noon and looked around for Koshi. I didn't see Koshi anywhere.

I moved the jeep around the corner and walked the half block back to the hotel's front entrance. Looking inside the lobby, I saw Koshi sitting on one of the couches. I walked over and sat down beside him.

"I have a duffle bag in my car for you. When we leave, you can walk with me and I'll drop it in the bushes for you," I said. "In the bag will also be the phone number of a partner of mine, Anthony Esposito, who you should call once all the armament is at your Virginia emporium. He will keep you informed on the date and place for physical delivery which will be in Leesburg, Virginia. Will that be a problem?" I asked.

"No sir," Koshi replied. "I've thrown in a few surprises for you, at no cost. I wanted you to know how much I appreciate your business. Mostly just flares, and some grenades and smoke incendiaries," Koshi added. With that, we exited the hotel. Walking to my jeep, I wondered who might be watching.

I looked around every dark hideaway as we walked. Once at the jeep, I reached into my vehicle and pulled out the duffle bag full of money. I dropped it into the bushes behind the rear end of the vehicle, and slowly climbed into the driver's seat. I gestured a salute to Koshi and pulled away.

Arriving back home, I pulled into the driveway of the hacienda and noticed my new-found homeless friend had spent the good part of the morning cleaning up the grounds from the hurricane. Tree branches were cut up and stacked off to the side. The one side of the hacienda that did sustain damage from the hurricane had its broken windows removed and was boarded up, and the rubble at the guard's shack was gone. Walking inside the house, I couldn't believe what I saw. Carlos had swept out all the water and debris from upstairs that covered the floor and had placed fans at various locations to help dry the floor. "You are fucking crazy," I said to Carlos, "but I like you."

"Carlos, I'm getting ready to do some traveling soon, so while I'm gone, you can stay here and continue working to clean up this place as my house guest."

"Sure thing boss," Carlos responded. "I'd like that. You won't recognize this place when you return. It will be like before the storm," Carlos replied.

"No, it won't," I responded sadly. "The love of my life won't be here."

Carlos apologized.

I knew Carlos didn't mean any harm. I told him I would be gone for several months, but I would return.

Chapter 13 – The Capture

With my first responsibility completed, it was time for me to begin the process of getting captured.

I walked to my room, and again brought out one of the burner phones. I made a call I was hesitant to make but had decided I had no other choice.

"Hap," I said with a fake cheerful voice. "It's Jason Williams, old buddy. How the hell are you?"

I used to see Hap's large yacht in Ft. Lauderdale often, when Hap would pull in to recruit young girls for his porn movie-making business.

"Wow, Jason Williams," Hap replied. "This is a surprise, hearing from you. You must be in trouble, my friend," Hap said as he let out a hearty laugh. "To what do I owe this pleasure?" he asked.

I dug deep for the courage to ask my next question. I knew Hap would contact authorities in the United States to advise them he was carrying cargo they might be interested in.

"Hap, I'm in trouble and I'd like to ask you for a favor. If you can help me out, I will be forever indebted to you, and that could be worth a lot," I continued.

"What do you need, my friend?" Hap asked. "I would be happy to help you with any problem you have."

"I'm currently in hiding from some very powerful people in the United States," I said. "I'm now in Cuba and I need you to sneak me back into the U.S., anywhere you can. Florida would be great or anywhere else your travels might bring you."

"That's it?" Hap replied. "I thought you'd want me to kill someone for you. No problem, Jason," he said. "I'm in Jamaica now and planning to head north in a day or two. Where exactly in Cuba are you?" he asked.

"Let's just say I'm on the southeastern part of the island. How about if you tell me where and when you can pick me up, and I will just meet you there," I said, not wanting to give up my location to a guy who would sell that info to the highest bidder.

"Jason," Hap laughed. "That's why I love you. You don't trust anyone. Let me take a quick look at the map, and let's see if we can put together some type of rendezvous. Okay," he said after a minute of searching, "I can be in the Marina Marlin Punta Gorda, or what's left of it, on Tuesday, around 8:00 A.M. Can we meet there?" Hap asked.

"That's perfect," I said. "Where will you be heading from there?"

Hap laughed again and replied, "Where do you want to go, my friend. I'm here to help you, so tell me your destination and I'll make sure you arrive there safe and sound," Hap continued.

Not wanting to give Hap any more information than I had to, I said, "How about Ft. Lauderdale, at the DoubleTree Hotel you often dock at?"

"Ah, I love that place," Hap replied. "Okay, you got it. See you on Tuesday," Hap laughed as he ended the call.

The following Tuesday, at exactly 8:00 A.M., I

arrived at what was left of the hotel's coffee shop and the Harbor Master's office at the Marina Marlin Punta Gorda. Most of the docks were empty, as those ships that usually dock there left before the hurricane hit.

I knew Hap would have to contact the Dock Master and check in once docking his yacht in the marina, so I just relaxed and waited.

Forty-five minutes later, I watched as Hap's 132', 2014 Benetti pulled into the marina and tied up along one of the long outside docks. I then waited for Hap to call into the Dock Master which he did about twenty minutes later. As he did, I got up and walked out from the coffee shop, heading down the rows of empty docks toward where Hap's yacht was mooring.

As I began to walk out along the docks, two Cuban police officers quietly ran up behind me and tackled me to the ground. Rolling on the wooden planks just a few feet above the water line, they pinned me down and cuffed me. I was stunned and had a moment of panic as they rolled me over causing me to almost fall into the water.

While lying on the dock, secured in cuffs, a

shadow appeared over me from a tall, well-dressed ex-CIA agent in dark sunglasses and an expensive Armani suit.

"Good to see you again Mr. Williams," the voice said in a very sarcastic tone. "You were not easy to find, but now that's water under the docks," he said as he laughed.

"You, my friend, are going to be detained under conditions detailed in the Patriot Act, on charges of murder and treason. You will immediately be sent to Gitmo, and you will not pass go," he said as he put his foot down on the back of my neck and pressed firmly down.

"And you'll stay there for as long as it takes for you to tell us all we need to know about who you're working with, and what plans you have."

He motioned for the two Cuban officers to stand me up and escort me back to his SUV. We drove the thirty minutes it took to arrive at the Southern Gate to the prison at Guantanamo Bay Cuba.

It didn't take long before they had me in chains. I was taken to detention camp #6, the worst and dirtiest of the six detention camps located on the base. A chain-link fence with concertina razor-sharp wire surrounded the deserted guard tower within Guantanamo's Camp Delta, a 612-unit unoccupied detention center.

"What the hell is going on here?" I yelled at the guard who was leading me back into solitary confinement. "I want my one phone call, and I want a lawyer," I demanded. "I am an American Citizen," I continued, "and I have rights. You need to let me speak to someone in charge."

I was taken to a back room where I was stripped naked. In the room were three men who's job it was to make sure I had no weapons or tracking devices on him.

When they finished searching my extremities, they had me put my fingers in my mouth and spread my lips open so they could see inside. Then I heard them say, "Now bend over, grab your ass cheeks and spread them open wide."

Seeing no visible evidence of hiding a weapon, or anything else, I was thrown an orange jumpsuit and told to put it on.

Two minutes later, the steel cage door slammed shut, and there was nothing but silence in my seven-foot by seven-foot cell. The only light was from a four inch by fifteen-inch window located at the bottom of the door.

Chapter 14 – Deal with the Devil

In order to get three-fourths of the States to ratify the approved resolution that would amend the U.S. Constitution, Granger Adams knew he'd have to make many deals, and some with those he wouldn't like.

Secretly, in return for Muslim allegiance to America, a deal was arranged between Granger Adams and Assam Bashula that no one else in *The Knights of Freedom* knew about.

His goal was to obtain an extremely large number of Muslims living in this country, *(up 200% in the last three years),* along with other immigrant groups, particularly from Latin America and Mexico, to help push these amendments through.

Granger had hoped by making this deal, other immigrant groups would want the same deal, and would also support the effort to ratify the joint resolution by the States.

In return for their support, Granger Adams agreed to create a new state within the new country known as the United Southern States of America. This new State would be created solely for Muslims.

The new State would be called "Haram" and would have the protections of the new USSA's Constitution. It would allow the State to rule according to Sharia Law.

This is the kind of deal President Bashula was hoping for. The Syrians were appalled the United States bombed their country for something they didn't do, and they were not happy the American President blamed them for sinking a cruise ship that killed over 4,000 innocent people, many of them women and children and some of whom were Muslim.

To pull this off, Bashula needed to unite as many of the Muslim Extremist leaders around the world as he could. He put out a call to all Muslim leaders in the battlefront nations of Iran, Afghanistan, Libya, and Somalia to meet with him in Saint-Denis, just north of Paris, to review the detailed plan he developed. That plan would allow Islamic Extremists to infiltrate the United States of America and put an end to the American infidels. It included setting up a number of sleeper cells in America and arming them with chemical weapons and a method of deploying them once he gave the word. His plan was to use drones to deliver the chemical agents.

He received unanimous support for his plan and full authority to lead a new attack on the United States of America.

The original idea of secretly migrating to the United States through Cuba via late night boatlifts had to be abandoned due to the new leadership of Cuba. During the first half of the current decade, the only path they had for entering the United States was through the Mexican border. Hiding amongst Mexican refugees, they would sneak across the border and meld into whatever city they could reach.

Their backup plan of hiding Jihadists inside caravans of migrating refugees from Honduras and other Central American countries to the United States also saw success.

Assam Bashula's new plan, however, was simple. He wanted the American infidels to become over-comfortable with the Muslim population that had worked its way into their cities, and he wanted Americans to begin to see Muslims more as Americans than as

Middle East immigrants. Quite a task if he could pull it off.

Bashula needed a cause for both sides to rally around. After deliberating with leaders of the NMWO, he decided that American Veterans and Granger Adams' push to approve his amendments, would be the path to take over the country he hated.

He called on "all" Muslims living in America to display their allegiance to America by donating their time and money to put an end to the homelessness experienced by American Veterans. This was a sensitive topic for most Americans.

Bashula asked every Muslim family to give at least ten hours per week of public service time to working with and helping Veterans that were homeless and/or disabled.

This gesture was met with open arms as the American public was overwhelmed by this generosity. American talking heads accepted this act of friendship and called for a peaceful coexistence with a group of people they grew up hating. Both sides embraced the act.

Bashula also requested all Muslims living in America publicly denounce the prior leaders of Iran and the New Muslim World Order and label them as extremists. He wanted them to publicly say these groups did not represent the true following of the Koran or the Muslim people.

Knowing well Americans would bolster their cause, it was hoped this declaration to officially support American Veterans, and to abandon their old Muslim lineage, would give an appearance *(however false)*, Muslims living in the United States of America were supportive of American policy and supportive of their American President, Bill McPherson.

Although this plan was farfetched and would be difficult to pull off, Granger Adams was not aware this was a façade orchestrated by the new Syrian leader.

Under Assam Bashula's plan, this new state, within time, would become the staging area for an end-all-attack on America. This attack would be unlike anything America had ever seen before. The attack would be led by Assam Bashula himself from within this country's own borders, specifically from inside their new State.

It was proposed this new State would be

about the size of Rhode Island, about a thousand square miles, and would be created from a small piece of land cut away from three existing southern states, *(North Carolina, South Carolina, and Tennessee).*

The attack would include the simultaneous detonation of chemical weapons on the West Coast of America. Assuming he could get them into the country, the attack would include over a hundred suicide bombers on the East Coast of America, let loose in Washington D.C. who would be on tour buses pretending to visit this nation's monuments and government facilities. They would take over the U.S. Government.

The main terror cell for this attack would be led by Josef Al-Hakim, a loyal Syrian who had already obtained entrance into the United States shortly after the retaliatory bombings that were orchestrated by the American President, Bill McPherson, three years ago.

Once Bashula was ready, Josef Al-Hakim would be set loose on the two nations creating havoc wherever he could. Josef Al-Hakim had already radicalized dozens of young Islamic extremists and by the time he was needed for the final battle, his army would be thousands strong, and capable of destroying the American infidels.

Chapter 15 – The Celebration

With their main adversary now locked away inside Cuba, there was confidence that America would now ratify the joint resolution approved by Congress.

To celebrate this, the *KOF* orchestrated an event just outside of their headquarters in Florida. The main speaker at this event was Granger Adams who was hoping to be the first president of the USSA.

The headquarters of the *KOF* was in an old rural area that was sometimes referred to by outsiders, as Hudson-tucky. It was well hidden, in the rural farmland and fenced in mobile home parks of Hudson, Florida, which is a small west coast town 40 miles northwest of Tampa, Florida along the Gulf of Mexico. It resembled what old Florida looked like a hundred years ago.

On this day, there was a massive party underway to celebrate the victory vote by the United States Congress that had been in the works for years.

The *KOF* had waged and won a battle on Capitol Hill very few knew was even being fought.

The timing of this celebration coincided with the two-month anniversary of the House of Representatives and the U.S. Senate approving the Joint Resolution initially outlining three amendments to the constitution.

Granger knew today's celebration was a little premature, but approval by three-fourths of the States was pretty much certain, due to the agreement he made with the Syrian President.

"My fellow countrymen," Granger Adams began. "This is a great moment in our history. This is a great moment in our time. This is a great moment in our world," he yelled to the crowd. Thunderous applause could be heard as what sounded like a thousand rifle shots were fired into the air.

"Sixty years ago, I dreamt of this day. During that time, I worked hard to achieve this goal. Now I can say to you that from this day forward, we will begin to live in a country not dominated by foreigners, liberals, and sanctuary cities. We will be governed by the beliefs that our forefathers instilled upon us. That, as landowners, we are the rulers of our land."

The crowd was now half-drunk from the free-flowing beer and booze, and from the euphoria of knowing they were standing on the forefront of a significant change in America.

"The United Southern States of America will be run by those that God created in his image," Granger told his audience. "Not by those that expect the government to take care of them, and not by those who don't work and plan to drain America dry," he continued.

Granger rallied the crowd for a good thirty minutes, basking in his own glory. Granger's mind was full of jubilation, and especially now that his adversary, and the only person who could possibly bring down all he's built, was locked away somewhere where no one would ever find him.

The only task that remained was to identify all those who were working with Jason Williams and bury them along with the man they just locked away for good. He and the rest of *The Knights of Freedom* would now relax and plan the growth of their new Union-of-States.

The changes he hoped to implement, to no one's surprise, would strip away many of the protections afforded to those that live off federal subsidies and welfare. Congressional leaders were signing up for this cause, mostly out of fear of being left out of any new government.

Granger had achieved what was never done before. He led the introduction of several joint resolutions to both the House and the Senate that would allow a way to easily make changes to the Constitution of the United States and not require ratification by the States. These resolutions were approved by Congress.

Now, if ratified by three-fourths of the States, these Joint Resolutions would allow Amendments to the Constitution to be adopted simply through authorization by the President of the United States.

Using his prepared talking points, Granger spelled out the three amendments to the crowd the *KOF* hoped would soon become part of the U.S. Constitution. They were:

Amendment-28. If adopted, would clarify wording previously recorded within the Constitution. Amendment-28 would read: *Any State could secede from the current United States of America by a majority vote of its own State government. It would no longer be bound by the current interpretation of the U.S. Constitution which appeared to prohibit States from seceding from the tyrannical rule of the U.S. Government. In addition, it would allow for a large pro-rated distribution of Federal dollars and military manpower to any State that did secede, thereby affording the new state protection from any other state attempting to take over the newly formed entity.*

Amendment-29. If adopted, would read: R*atification by the States to approve a change to the Constitution would no longer be required. Amendments could be approved by the President of the United States if brought forward by approval of a joint resolution from Congress.*

Amendment-30. If adopted, *would repeal Amendment-22, which limits a President of the United States to only two terms. This new amendment gives a President the ability to serve unlimited terms in office.*

It had taken a long time to arrive at this historic moment, but finally, history was about to be made thanks to the efforts of *The Knights of Freedom*. The *KOF* had control of the States' Governors along with large masses of population within each state and felt extremely confident they could get the three-fourths of the States needed to ratify these new amendments.

As expected, the vote by the House and the Senate was so controversial the opposition to this vote demanded it immediately be brought before the United States Supreme Court for an assessment of its legality. A decision by the SCOTUS was expected shortly.

Granger Adams' first group of states to secede was already in place and was planning to recreate the south as it once was. He knew they were tired of being bullied by what they felt were northern bleeding-heart liberals. This first group of eleven states planning to secede had already prepared for this outcome by petitioning the Federal Government to become the United Southern States of America (USSA).

Dazed by the applause of the crowd, and there were thousands of exuberant supporters all chanting his name, Granger Adams took a moment and stared out into space, thinking back to his childhood days when he was on his dad's farm in southern Georgia. He could see it as if it were yesterday:

Granger ended his speech to his loyal followers with the phrase, "The south shall rise again," as the crowd began chanting that phrase back to him, over and over.

Chapter 16 – Gitmo

I was not a happy camper being stuck here at Guantanamo. During my first seven days of captivity, the only human I saw was a guard who brought me food once a day, and a worker who came every other day to escort me out to a field where I could empty my port-o-potty.

Sometimes, they wouldn't show up, or they'd skip a day or two before letting me empty the container housing my urine and excrement. That was probably the dirtiest and smelliest job I had done since my early days with the Secret Service.

Each day when my food was brought to me, I would demand I be given legal representation and an opportunity to make a phone call. The soldier bringing my meals said he would pass my request along to his superiors, but nothing ever came from that.

Locked in my cell, I was in a world unto myself, where quiet and emptiness was all there was, and despair seeped into my bones and eventually my mind.

Within my seven-by-seven cell, I would go from corner to corner and try to count the inches. I would do this while sitting on the floor. Then I would stand and slide my hand along the wall, again counting the inches. I was trying to do whatever I could to pass the time.

I would stretch out both hands and try to touch the wall on both at the same time. Then I would laugh since I was not quite able to accomplish this. The ceiling was less than a foot above my head and my metal bed took up half the room.

Hour after hour, it was total isolation. The cell I was in was dark most of the time, but at a certain time of the day, the sun would enter the cell for about thirty minutes. Just enough time for me to make marks on the wall.

I was really getting smelly and I was becoming grungy looking with a beard that was probably an inch long now. Being kept here was beginning to squeeze the sanity from my mind and the spirit from my soul. I was afraid if I began thinking back on my life, it would be all over for me.

By the tenth day in isolation, I had stopped

asking about my rights and just tried to hold on to my sanity by making a mark on the wall for each day I was being held. Each morning I would scratch a line on the wall. Later in the day when the sun provided me with some light, I would lengthen the mark, from a two-inch-line to a four-inch line. This is what I was taught to do while in Secret Service training. This training was about keeping my mind intact. It gave me something to look forward to each day.

I knew the CIA oversaw prisoners held here in Guantanamo, and not the military. The military was strictly providing guard service only. And I knew the CIA was working for *The Knights of Freedom*, so getting out of here was not something that would occur without the help of Dylan Rains.

After twenty-one days of isolation, someone came into my cell, hosed it down with me in it, and then took me to an interrogation room a few hundred yards away.

The only items in that room were a chair, which I was immediately strapped into, and a light dangling from a wire reaching down to within a foot of my head. Upon arriving there, I again demanded my rights as an

American citizen, but those requests just fell on deaf ears.

My interrogators were only interested in finding out who worked with me, and where could they be found. They questioned me for what seemed like hours on end, trying to get me to identify who else was involved in my plan to destroy *The Knights of Freedom*.

My captors knew their interrogation was useless. They knew I would never betray my friends. Their goal, however, was to break my spirit and to break my mind. They felt if they couldn't get me to expose who was working with me, they could at least break me enough that I would just basically become a vegetable and unable to continue my pursuit of their organization.

It wouldn't be long before they began physical torture, and I wasn't looking forward to that. In the meantime, after each multi-hour interrogation session, I was brought back to my cell in solitary confinement.

After a while, they began to use sleep deprivation techniques as a weapon against me. Almost every night, and often during the day, they would make loud sounds outside my cell. They would even pound on my cell door to ensure I would wake up. They then tried every torture method known to them to determine who was working with me to bring down the *KOF*.

According to the number of marks on the wall, it had only been a few weeks, so this was just a walk in the park, I thought. But privately, I knew I was losing a grip on reality, and I might not be able to hold out much longer.

After thirty days of isolation, I was being humiliated in front of local Cuban workers brought over to the prison-side of the base.

The guards would strip me naked and threaten to rape me in front of these soldiers, both male and female. A couple of these workers were perverted sex offenders, and they personally tried to reach out and touch me.

It was humiliating to have these soldiers, and sometimes other prisoners on the base, gawking at me. And some of the perverts could be heard groaning sounds of passion as they stared at me. And often, they would just beat me while hanging naked. They even used drills and other cutting tools to hurt me but to no avail. I would not talk.

I was extremely weak from a lack of proper food and water, and my body was beginning to react to this condition with the dry heaves.

I felt like I had lost around 15 pounds and looked severely dehydrated. Sometimes I went days without water, or any kind of liquid and it was affecting my ability to urinate. I didn't know how much longer I could hold on. I hoped the plan they put together at the hacienda was working and they would be coming to rescue me soon.

The worst came when I was given several bags of IV fluid, after removing the port-o-potty from my room. My urine and crap ended up all over the floor that I had to walk on.

I was close to a breaking point and was even beginning to worry I might never get out of this hell hole. I thought to myself, "Where the hell is Dylan Rains?"

On the forty-fifth day of my captivity, based on orders directly from Phillip Henderson, guards tied my hands behind my back and brought me out into the courtyard. One of the guards was holding a four-foot-long broom handle, and I knew exactly what they planned to do with it. As they inserted the handle, I passed out from the pain and was later returned to my cell. The crowd that watched the event, cheered as I fell to the ground.

While in the courtyard, what I didn't know was my guards had filled my cell with snakes.

I was deathly afraid of snakes, so when I was awakened by a slithering feeling on my neck, my panic told me this could be the breaking point.

The next day, I had finally reached the maximum I could take when electricity was used to stop and start my heart. For me, the pain had become unbearable.

Finally, on the fifty-first day of my captivity, I received a personal visit from Phillip Henderson, the ex-CIA agent who captured me at the Marina inside Cuba almost two months ago.

Phillip was sent down to Gitmo, to put the final nail in my coffin. He was told I had reached the end of the line, and it appeared I was ready to talk or die. Phillip was there to provide one final mental anguish against me.

Phillip entered my cell and said in a slow and clear voice, "Your daughter Teresa gave you up to *The Knights of Freedom*. She owed an exceptionally large sum of money to the man she is now sleeping with, Granger Adams," Phillip told me. "And it was her," Phillip laughed as he continued, "who provided us with information on how to locate your hacienda, and when you'd be home and not traveling. She gave us all the information we needed to find you."

"Only problem was, you weren't there when we came for you," Phillip continued. "So, we had to take your wife instead. I heard they had some real fun with her," Phillip smiled. "Heard she is, or was one hot bitch," Phillip continued.

I squirmed and moaned as the pain of hearing this was too much to handle. "You bastards," I cried. "You didn't have to hurt her. I would have traded my soul for her freedom."

Phillip then told me of the CIA undercover agent, Carlos, they planted at his hacienda.

“He was the one that gave us the heads up on you being at the marina in Punta Gorda that morning.

So, you see Jason, you were easy to find, once we had an idea where you had disappeared to,” Phillip continued. “And your family,” he told Jason, “they don’t really care about you. You should know they feel your wife’s death was your fault.” With what little remained of his mind, I began begging for mercy.

Phillip was enjoying the pain that the weakened, bent over and crippled body that lay before him was in. He decided to thrust one more pain upon me by telling me my buddy Dylan Rains had been killed while snooping around the base this morning. “Shot by one of the Marine guards,” he told me. “I’ll get you a picture of his body, so you can identify the remains,” Phillip said as he laughed.

I stopped breathing for a moment. I could not believe my ears. I gasped for air and broke down as I listened to Phillip’s words. “No, no,” I said as I lowered my head. I yelled at Phillip to stop saying those things, but those requests fell on deaf ears.

I moaned and screamed as I realized I would never get out of here. I had finally been broken.

Chapter 17 – Change Happens

While Jason was incarcerated, and without waiting for ratification on this vote, President Bill McPherson publicly honoured Granger Adams for his leadership in this important historic change.

As his reward, POTUS appointed Granger Adams, the USSA's constitutional author. He was tasked with forming a new government body and a new constitution within the next ninety days. In the meantime, the anticipated newly amended U.S. Constitution would serve as his guiding direction until a replacement document could be created internally.

The Knights of Freedom was the group clearly responsible for achieving this goal. Hence, the celebration that just occurred in Pasco County, Florida. It was estimated that over 10,000 of the KOF's followers attended the festivities up at the Veterans Memorial Park located on Hicks Road in the middle of Hudson, Florida.

As Granger began drafting the new constitution, its first article stated that a reciprocal arrangement would exist between the USSA and the USA, for sharing the facilities of Guantanamo Bay, Cuba.

The Supreme Court of the United States had convened an emergency session to rule on the constitutionality of the recent Joint Resolution which was just approved by Congress.

The question at hand was not whether the correct process was followed in approving the Joint Resolution, but what the result of such an act would be if allowed to stand.

It essentially would mean the end of the United States of America as we knew it. And the court knew that their role in this decision was to preserve the country our forefathers created when they created the Constitution. The decision in their opinion was simple.

However, the laws of the land had not been broken. The will of the people, through their representatives in the nation's capital, voted their minds. Until a law was not interpreted correctly, SCOTUS had no choice but to allow the vote to stand. It would be up to the States to decide if this became a reality.

The next morning, every newspaper in the country led off with the headline:

"SCOTUS RULES RESOLUTION IS CONSTITUTIONAL"

There was not one member of *The Knights of Freedom* that could be reached on the phone that morning. Those in leadership positions within the KOF were all huddled inside the White House looking for acknowledgment from the President of the United States, and from Granger Adams, that the resolution would now be up to the States. They wanted a timetable set, and if not met, their vote would be counted as not opposing.

They wanted POTUS to make a statement supporting their victory in Congress, and demand that the States vote on this issue, or pass on voting, within the next thirty days.

After hearing the opinion of the Supreme Court, eleven States submitted legal papers to their respective State's governing bodies, requesting that their sovereign borders be recognized as part of the USSA once it becomes established.

These were the same eleven states that seceded prior to the civil war. They were

Alabama, Florida, Georgia, Louisiana, Mississippi, South Carolina, Texas, Arkansas, North Carolina, Tennessee, and Virginia.

The legal papers stated that once the USSA was created, it would establish Nashville, Tennessee as its Capital. The physical location would be in the Tennessee Secretary of State's office complex which was across the street from the State Capitol building.

Granger Adams announced the first five articles of the new Constitution for the United Southern States of America:

> **Article 1:** Ownership of Prisoners. Landowners that provide proof of land ownership would be allowed to purchase farm workers from the State or Federal Prison System. Safeguards would be established to ensure that purchased farm workers did not escape and deposits would be lost should this occur.
>
> **Article 2:** Federal Law vs. State Law. Laws of the State will override Federal Laws. No Federal Law will be rendered legal if it conflicts with any State law within the USSA.

Article 3: Sovereignty of State. Each of the eleven states of the USSA and the new Muslim state of Haram will have the authority to govern itself and will have the authority to create its own laws and elect its own government.

Article 4: Security of Borders. Each state will be allowed to protect and control who is allowed entry.

Article 5: Limited Immigration. Each state will establish the number of immigrants it will allow entry each year. Each state will control its own immigration policies. These policies could be changed at any time.

Mass confusion was predominant throughout the two Americas. An exodus of unproportioned amounts was occurring both into and from these eleven states. Property was being bought at extremely low prices and some were being sold for extremely high prices. It just came down to how badly folks wanted in or out of a state.

The boundaries of the new Muslim State of Haram were being worked out in the Tennessee capital, in accordance with the agreement Granger Adams signed months ago.

Chapter 18 – The United-Six

(This chapter was completely written by my 16-year-old grandson)

It was early morning when the United-Six took off from Antonio Maceo Airport in a Blackhawk UH-60 helicopter, provided by one of Dylan's friends. This was the team Dylan brought in to find and free his friend Jason Williams.

After a thirty-five-minute flight, they arrived at their planned landing area, a mile short of the southeast gate of the detention center at Guantanamo Bay, Cuba. Once there, they unloaded their weapons and all their gear from the Blackhawk and marched east one mile, toward the base.

The team was being led by Rachel Lynch. The government file on the team's leader read as follows:

Name:	Rachel "Mute" Lynch
DOB:	10/22/1997 Tampa, Florida
Height:	5'5"
Weight:	184 lbs.
Description:	Kick Ass Fighter
Race/Skin tone:	Caucasian
Hair Style:	Short and straight
Hair Color:	Black
Eye Color:	Blue

Rachel was raised by Irish parents in Tampa, Florida. When she turned twenty, she joined the Tampa Tactical Force (TTF), and mastered the art of assassination and stealth. After five years, she decided to leave the TTF and become a contracted mercenary working for anyone who would pay her price. Our government found out what she was doing and captured her. Instead of sending her off to a life sentence in prison, she was placed in the United States' most elite special forces group called "The United-Six."

Rachel Lynch took point and spotted a lone guard standing outside, unaware of what was about to happen. She darted toward him and shoulder tackled him, falling hard to the ground. As they fell to the ground, she grabbed her knife from her boot holster and held it up against his neck.

Rachel Lynch was code-named "Mute" for her ability to sneak past enemies unnoticed. She and her partners in the United-Six were all well-trained assassins.

"¿Dónde está Jason? Dímelo ya o despídete de todo," she said interrogating the man as to where Jason Williams was being held.

He told her where Jason was located but said to her that she'd need him to lead her there. *"llévanos con él,"* she told him, as he stood up quickly and started to lead the extraction team to Jason. At least that's what they hoped he was doing.

The guard took them to his jeep, where he said to Rachel, *"Se llevaron a Jason al Campo Delta 6. Está lejos pero no en auto."* Luckily, Rachel was fluent in Spanish and could understand what the guard was telling her.

"He's in Camp Delta in Camp #6," she relayed back to the group. "He said it's easier to drive instead of walk."

A few minutes later, the United-Six team arrived at Camp Delta. *"Por favor, amigos, por aquí,"* he said.

"Rachel," one of the other team members said, "ask him if he can speak English?"

"Hablas inglés?" she said to the guard.

"¡Sí! Pero apenas es entendible," he responded.

Rachel replied and interpreted, "Yes, he can, he said, but it's barely understandable," she paraphrased.

“Well shit, there goes that” another team member could be heard muttering.

The Cuban guard led the team to a staircase that went down through a long tunnel and into Camp #6. There was a sign on the wall that read: Solitary Confinement.

“Oh my God,” one of the team members said, “Jason is being held in Solitary Confinement?”

“I guess so, if he’s leading us to Jason then yes, yes he is,” answered Rachel.

“Aquí está el celular del señor Jason,” the guard said. *“Ábrelo, lentamente, no queremos que la gente sepa que estamos aquí,”* said Rachel. *“Sí, sí, por supuesto,”* responded the guard.

His hands were shaking as he put the key in the lock and opened the door, slowly and quietly.

As the door opened, you could see that there was a crumpled, and very ratty looking individual coiled down in the corner of the cell.

“The man looks like he’s been to hell and back without supplies for the trip,” Rachel thought to herself. His hair was long and strangely, and his beard looked like it was a nest for cockroaches. He was hunched over and could have easily passed for an ISIS Jihadist.

"Jason?" a voice from the back of the team asked quietly.

Not recognizing the voice, I shouted back without looking to see who was there, "What do you want now? Just leave me alone," I said as I turned my head toward the team.

My eyes almost bulged out of my head as I jumped up after seeing who it was. "Dylan, you're... you're alive," I said softly.

"Yep, it's me bud," Dylan responded. "We're getting you out of this fucking hell hole."

Just then a man wearing a black suit walked up and headed in the direction of Jason's' cage.

"What the fuck is going on here?" he shouted. He didn't notice Rachel slowly creeping up behind him with her knife in hand. She grabbed him and held the knife to his neck.

"You obviously speak English, so, who are you, asshole?" she shouted at him. "You have five seconds before the last thing you see is all your blood spilling onto the floor, and a giant slash in your neck," she said. *Rachel is good at interrogating people.*

"Phillip Henderson," the man responded. "I'm in charge of this prisoner."

"No, he means he's the asshole who pushed me to the ground, threw handcuffs on me, and told me I'm being arrested for the murder of my wife. He's the guy who threw me in here," yelled Jason in a fit of rage. "Kill him," I yelled to Rachel.

"Rachel, take him outside and make sure he doesn't leave. We'll be out soon," Jason Ramsburg, the United-Six Commander, jumped in and said to her.

Rachel nodded and said to Phillip Henderson, "Come on asshole," still holding that knife to his neck. She's pretty pissed, and it wouldn't take much for her to move her knife a little and slit his neck. However, she honored her Commander's wish as they both just walked away. As Rachel and Phillip left the cell, I was helped to my feet and escorted out of the dark cell I had been living in for over two months.

Chapter 19 – Going Home

The United-Six rescue of Jason, although it took longer than they had originally thought, worked perfectly. By breaching a wall at the southeast gate, and sneaking up on a security guard, they were able to make the guard take Dylan and his team to the cell they were holding Jason in.

After Dylan helped Jason to his feet, they walked him outside into the courtyard for some fresh air and a chance to see the sun for the first time in months. Both Dylan and Rachel noticed red blood stains on the backside of his orange jumpsuit, around the rectum area and knew immediately what they had done to him. Rachel thought to herself that Phillip would need to suffer the same act himself.

But first, following Dylan's orders, the United-Six took Phillip aside and had him make a call to Granger Adams.

"Granger, it's Phillip," he was told to say. "I wanted to let you know that my last interrogation of Jason Williams went a little too far, and I'm afraid we overdid it, sir. He's dead," Phillip said against his will. "We're going to dump this guy out at sea if that's okay with you?" he asked.

"You tried your best to do what you needed to do," was Granger Adams' only words to Phillip, and the last words Phillip would ever hear.

Two members of the United-Six then took Phillip Henderson away for good. On the way out, they grabbed the broomstick that was laying on the ground outside of Jason's cell and showed Phillip how it feels to receive a rectal implant from a foreign object.

They then took him outside the gate and tied him to a tree in the woods, about half-a-mile from the base. They knew the critters would have a feast of him once their smell latched onto his bloody trail. And then the bears and the wolves would decide at night, which one of them got the bigger piece of this poor excuse for a human.

Back at the base, Dylan contacted the Base Commander, Hollis Grant, and using Secret Service protocol, set up a private meeting at the Commander's office.

They hosed me down as best they could and got me into a clean set of sweatpants before bringing me to Hollis Grant's office.

The meeting between Dylan, Hollis Grant, and myself was private and held in the tightest of security. Dylan brought me to Hollis's office, so he could see I was in fact, alive and sort of well. He made sure no one else had seen him bringing me there.

The Commander knew he could be put on trial for treason for what he was doing, but he loved his country way too much to allow it to be railroaded by politicians. Once inside, Dylan brought Hollis up to date on what had just occurred, and what the plan would be going forward.

I was to be pronounced dead by the base Commander, Hollis Grant, and then placed on board the next naval vessel that was departing for Norfolk Virginia.

I could barely stand up but was able to enter the cell phone number of the President of the United States, Bill McPherson, using a secure line provided to me by the base Commander.

"Bill," I began. "It's me, Jason Williams. Contrary to what you may have heard from those you work with, I am alive. I have been held captive for almost three months at Gitmo and was kept in solitary confinement all of that time at the request of Granger Adams, your buddy," I said with a sarcastic tone to it.

"Oh my God, Jason, I just heard you were dead," Bill said in a shocked but happy voice. "Granger told me you had been in a boating accident and your body was never recovered. I am truly glad to hear that is not true. I know you do not approve of my role in *The Knights of Freedom*, but I only associated myself with them to ensure the reelection of my campaign. You believe me, don't you Jason," Bill said as honestly as he could.

"Bill," I said in a firm but weak authoritative voice, "you cannot tell anyone I am still alive. I need to remain dead in the eyes of the *KOF*. If there is any possible chance for us to reconcile, I need to know I can still trust you."

"Right now," I continued, "I need you to do something for me. I need you to send an email from your official account to the Base Commander at Gitmo. The email must request that my body be returned back to the United States as quickly as possible and that it be turned over to the CIA, upon its arrival in Norfolk, Virginia," I demanded.

"Can you do that for me?" I asked. "If you show your trust in me now, it'll go a long way toward forgiving your actions and participation in having me incarcerated," he added.

"That email will go out in the next twenty minutes," Bill told Jason. "I'll get my Chief of Staff, Garrett Johnson, to get right on it. I hope you can forgive me and we can make a very bad situation better," Bill concluded.

"No! You can't let anyone else know of this email. It must be sent directly from you to Hollis Grant. No copies anywhere else," I told Bill.

"Okay Jason, I will do as you ask. Just remember I am helping you with whatever you are planning," Bill said.

"Thanks, Bill. I will be waiting here for your email to arrive and will contact you once back in the United States," I said as we ended the call.

Hollis had arranged for the U.S.S. Tequesta, an Armored Cruiser (CA), which had just brought supplies down to the base, to transport the corpse of Jason Williams back to the United States. Hollis informed the ship's captain that a government team from the CIA would meet him when he docked in Norfolk to take custody of the casket that would soon be loaded onto his ship.

He also informed the Captain that the body of the deceased would be accompanied by U.S. Marine 2nd Lieutenant, Samantha "Sam" Wilkinson, and during the two-day trip, she would have full authority over her cargo.

Within ten minutes, Hollis forwarded those orders to the ship's captain along with the President's email, which contained the Presidential Seal. The ship's captain accepted his new orders from the President of the United States.

That afternoon, a color guard along with Hollis Grant accompanied the shrouded casket of Jason Williams below deck onto the U.S.S. Tequesta. Alongside of Hollis Grant was 2nd Lieutenant Samantha Wilkinson. Jason's body was brought to a locked storage/supply room. This room was always kept locked due to the number of drugs that were stored on board for medical reasons. It was located two decks below, and at the stern of the ship.

When no one was around, Lt. Wilkinson would bring food from the mess hall in her purse to secretly provide some food and drink to me.

Each day of the two-day journey from Guantanamo Bay to Norfolk, Samantha made five or six trips below deck to ensure the well-being of her cargo. Each visit down to the supply room, she made sure I had enough to eat and drink. And that I was able to utilize a portable latrine as needed.

Although seeking solitude, I felt comfortable around Samantha Wilkinson, as she was a very consoling factor for him. She had soft looking blue eyes, with straight blonde and brunette hair colors, although you couldn't tell much since she had to wear her hair rolled up on top of her head and inside her hat.

She didn't look like she should be in a Marine uniform. She was the new breed of Marine, younger, prettier, and much thinner than what you'd expect a Marine to be. I was always glad when she came below deck to see him.

When Samantha held his hand, to aid him during his bouts with depression, he felt comfortable. He didn't think of her sexually, but rather as a family member trying to be of help. There was nothing sexual he thought he would ever feel again after what they did to him at Gitmo.

I drew comfort from Sam's caring touch and companionship. She was a nurse, and although his first day at sea was a rough one, on the second day of their journey, I felt I was coming back from the dead. She treated me medically as I had many wounds and infections.

With just a few hours remaining before the U.S.S. Tequesta would arrive at its destination, Samantha came down to the supply/storage room with a fresh set of clothes.

She had begun to like this broken man and she wanted to help him in any way she could. I knew I was now going to recover. And I knew I owed a lot of it to her.

At approximately 0600 on the third day of his journey back to the United States, the U.S.S. Tequesta pulled into Berth 5-6, at the Norfolk

Naval Base in Norfolk, Virginia. Secure lines were put in place as the ship was tied down and the boarding ramps were placed in their proper positions. The first one was placed at the front of the ship, and then another ramp was placed at the rear of the ship. The front ramp was for officers and dignitaries to exit or return to the ship. The rear ramp was for the crew.

To the surprise of the ship's crew, the boatswain mate blew the captain's whistle which was immediately followed by the Officer-on-Deck signaling the okay for the Vice President of the United States to come on board.

After the obligatory salutes, Douglas Williams met with the Captain of the ship, as he went through the process of turning his cargo over to the VP's Marine Honor Guard of six official looking Marines. "I was told to turn the body over to the CIA, but I guess you out-rank them, sir," the Captain said.

Within minutes of docking, Jason's casket, with the aid of the color guard that accompanied the Vice President, was removed from the U.S.S. Tequesta, and transferred to the back of a waiting hearse. With two government SUV's in front of the hearse and two behind it, Jason was on his way to Leesburg Virginia, to the set of farmhouses Anthony had purchased for them.

Once off the Naval Base, they pulled over and I emerged from the casket I was in and took the entire back seat of the hearse to stretch out.

The drive took almost four hours, which included parts of I-95 through Richmond to the 495 beltway that circles Washington D.C., and then out route seven, past Reston and finally through suburban developments and open farmlands.

The Vice President's limo, followed by the hearse, drove directly into the large garage at the farmhouse on top of the hill, while his entourage remained out front.

The charade of the century appeared to be working. Jason arrived at the smaller farmhouse, which was located at the top of the hill. I was looking shabby, and unshaven, and extremely weak.

Dylan and Douglas helped me from the car and up the ramp leading into the house and over to the kitchen table where I could sit free for the first time in several months.

They fixed me a coffee, but I demanded a Jack Daniels instead. After downing two shots of JD, I said I needed and wanted a shower.

Helping him upstairs and into the bathroom off the master bedroom, it was almost ninety minutes before Jason came downstairs to meet his rescuers. I could barely walk.

Dylan Rains and Jason's brother Douglas wrapped their arms around me and just stood there for a full minute before letting me sit down. "Well, my brother," Douglas said as he held me tight, "you have been through a lot.

"Let's just go slow so you can come to grips with being free of that hell hole. How about some breakfast, along with some hot coffee and then we can begin to bring you up-to-date?" he asked.

"I'm not hungry," I responded. The house staff had prepared bacon and eggs for me, but I wasn't ready to eat yet. I did drink the coffee with lots of cream and sugar, however.

"I picked at the bacon and then sat back and thanked the two greatest true friends a man could have. Even if one was my brother, I knew these two were also friends.

"What an ordeal," I said as I let out a giant sigh of relief. "I can't begin to put into words, what it was like being at Gitmo. The torture was like what I had heard they did to enemy combatants. I don't think I could have lasted another week. I don't know what I would have told them, to get them to end the torture," I said as my emotions began to flow.

I looked past the two men I was chatting with and looked out into the living room, where sitting on the couch was a familiar face with a familiar smile. It was Samantha, who was chatting with Anthony.

When she saw me looking at her, she rose from the couch in the living room and walked over to where I was sitting. She then reached out her hand and shook mine with great pride.

"You are a brave man, and a true American hero my friend," she said in a caring tone. "I wish you the best of luck with your future endeavors and know that I am available for you whenever you need me," she said as she saluted me. She gave me her phone number and said to call her whenever I needed to talk with someone. She then excused herself and left the room and the farmhouse.

I watched her get into one of Douglas's SUV's and leave. I hoped I'd get to thank her again, sometime in the future.

Chapter 20 – Coming up to Speed

The first few nights at the farmhouse were rough as I continued to have recurring nightmares from my time in Gitmo.

I knew I would need help, both physically and mentally, from the trauma caused by an almost three-month incarceration at that hell hole. I tried to stay close to Douglas and to Dylan and to talk as much to them as I could in hopes of regaining my mental capacities.

What I did do a lot, was drink alcohol. I was consuming almost half a bottle of Jack Daniels every night. It was the only thing that helped me sleep.

Almost a week had passed before I would go outside and sit on the small front porch of the cabin up the hill. I forced myself to open the door and venture a few feet out, but I was fearful my captors would see me there and beat me again, as they had done several nights a week while in captivity.

Eventually, Dylan and Douglas were able to sit with me, allowing me to talk about being held in a seven by seven-foot cell. After two weeks at the farmhouse, they all began to laugh about Jason's captivity. I was beginning to become my old self again.

Finally, after three weeks of freedom, I was ready to be brought up-to-speed on the status of our battle against *The Knights of Freedom*.

I had gained some of the weight back I lost, and my appetite was on the rise. My hair was cut into a neatly trimmed marine haircut and I was clean-shaven. I was ready.

"Except for your incarceration, everything we planned has gone like clockwork," Douglas said as he looked at Jason. "We've been able to identify where the *KOF* keep their funds, and how to get at it. We've figured out their organizational structure and identified who does what. And we've planted bugs into all their software, so we can begin hacking their accounts. We're ready to begin the take-down of the *KOF* once you give the word," he said to me

Douglas jumped in, "Right now, Granger Adams still thinks you are dead. He no longer feels any concern you might try to stop him. With his guard down, I think it is the perfect time to strike," he continued. "As for the plans of the *KOF*, not much has changed from a few months ago," Douglas said.

"*The Knights of Freedom* are still out to bring down the United States of America as we know it. Once they create their Union-of-States, they will plan to rule every individual under their control. They plan to establish a new government that endorses the old ways of the south, in the south."

"They have gotten the Supreme Court to acknowledge their Joint Resolution is constitutional, and they are about to implement their plan to change the U.S. Constitution," Dylan added.

"There are two things that have changed, however, since you were taken to Gitmo," Douglas said. "The first is the *KOF* now has momentum, and they are gaining a long list of supporters. Over half the State's Governors have already announced they will vote to accept these changes to our Constitution. And a dozen more are leaning that way."

"And what is the second?" I asked.

"Although the States have not yet ratified these changes, the *KOF* is moving to implement them. They may get so far into this that it will be impossible to unwind their efforts even if they don't get the three-fourths ratification that they need," Douglas responded. "It may be too late to stop them."

Douglas stared at Jason and said, "We need to begin an effort to change the minds of those States that are in the camp of the *KOF*. And that won't be easy as the word on the street is that many of these states are being pressured by their constituents to ratify these amendments." Douglas continued, "We're hearing that a large base made up of Muslims along with a number of Latin communities are demanding their state ratify these amendments.

"And then we need to take out Granger Adams."

Sipping some coffee, I offered my thoughts. "Let's plan to let the deception continue for at least another week. That will give me time to regain my focus, strength, and energy. Then we'll move toward the elimination of *The Knights of Freedom*. I need to get my head straight before we take any action.

"You said you have been able to ascertain how they get their financial support and where it resides, so I presume we can shut it down without much delay?" I asked them both but looked directly at Dylan.

"Yes, we have all of their bank accounts flagged and ready to be closed electronically. My tech guys are standing by and waiting for me to give the order to shut them down. Without cash or credit, they will be immobile and powerless," Dylan said as he smiled. This was the part of his assignment Dylan loved the most. If it had to do with computers and hacking.

"Okay, sounds like you've all been busy. It made my stay at Gitmo worthwhile," I responded. "The guns should be here within a few days. I'll check with Koshi later this afternoon.

"And although I may not be thinking clearly right now, I can assure you there is one son-of-a-bitch I will personally be taking out. Right or wrong," I said as I stood up and headed back upstairs.

"Where are you going?" Douglas asked.

At the top of the stairs, I stopped and said looking down at my two saviors, "You guys are incredible. My incarceration did not happen in vain," I added. "But now I need to go lay down again. I may not be back down for several hours, but I trust that will give you two time to contact Justin and bring him in from the cold. He needs to be here, and you'll need to bring him up to speed," I said.

Anthony agreed and said he'd arrange to fly Justin down here immediately.

"Just give me a few more hours of uninterrupted sleep. Then, I think we'll be ready to move," I said as I slowly limped to the master bedroom. "Night all," I said as I waved a thumbs-up to them.

Half the day had passed when I was awakened by the smell of ribs soaked in bourbon cooking on the grill. Now fully awake, I jumped into the shower, dressed, and made my way back downstairs.

"Have you guys been sitting around all day waiting for me to wake up?" I asked with a bit of humor in my tone.

"We didn't want to make any noise that might cause you to get up before you were ready," Dylan said. "But time is flying by, so let's get some food in you and continue our Phase-2 discussion," he said with a smile.

Looking at Jason, Douglas said, "We have several campaigns that can begin as soon as you give the word. First, we have outlined a smear campaign against the *KOF* on several of the social media sites. Using their Charter, which Dylan was able to get us a copy of, we have created a dozen negative ads that discredit what they stand for," Douglas said. "We will saturate the internet social media sites with this information."

"The second part of the social media blitz against them will consist of sexist statements that will highlight their misogynistic stand. "These statements will be made to look as if they came directly from Granger Adams," Douglas said.

These statements will show he sees women as second-class citizens and his eventual plan is to amend their Constitution to say women must obey their men," he continued. "It will be like their position on owning slaves," Douglas said in a clear and direct voice.

Anthony immediately broke in with, "We also have proof of what they have done with some of the money they have raised," he said. "We know they've lined their own pockets with cash, and they've transferred much of it to offshore bank accounts. We will document all this and put it out on the internet as well," he continued.

And then with a smile and a proud tone in his voice, Anthony continued, "And the coup d'état is that we have documented proof Granger has used a portion of these funds he's collected to personally buy large pieces of property inside the eleven states that will be seceding from the union. I even have documented proof he used *KOF* money to buy a 2500-acre plantation down in Georgia, which is now in his name. It not only contains a ten-bedroom mansion, but it has an airfield and a large hangar located on the property as well."

"Wow, this is pretty damaging stuff," I said as I moved my empty plate of ribs away. "I think this social media attack should discredit all of them enough that it might cause an uprising of the American people who will question whether what the *KOF* is doing is in their best interests or not," I said.

"Dylan, you said you were able to identify who the key players are within the *KOF*?" I asked.

"You bet," he replied with a smile. "I have the names of two high ranking Senate Intelligence Committee members that are officially supporting the *KOF*. They are Senator Kokingham from Minnesota and Senator Harold Rosen from Arizona," Dylan responded.

"However, they have been in the Senate for decades, and they've built up a strong base of supporters. The only way I see to remove them from the picture is to physically take them out," Dylan said. "We have been watching these two key *KOF* members for over a month now and know their every routine.

"We know what time they come and go from home, and where and when they go out to eat. They will be easy to take out," Dylan said in an assuring voice. "I can have the United-Six take positions at several different locations throughout the United States, and we can plan to eliminate these two *KOF* members simultaneously once you give the order," he said looking at me.

Chapter 21 – Getting Ready

Half-a-dozen ZKZM-700A handheld laser assault rifles arrived in three different U-Haul trucks over the next few days. The weapons were lightweight and came with telescopic sights and extra lithium mini batteries.

Everything I ordered was there, including an RPG I had talked about but didn't order. It was a gift from Koshi, along with a card inside that read: 'go get em'.

I had not shown my face outside the farmhouse for several weeks for fear of being spotted. I felt comfortable no one knew I was still alive, and what I was planning. I decided to take a chance and use one of the new burner phones to make a call I had been thinking about making for weeks now.

"Hi, this is Teresa," the voice on the other end of the phone said, not knowing who was calling.

"Hello Teresa," I said, resulting in total silence on the other end of the line.

Teresa responded, “Who is this?”

“It’s me, your Dad,” I responded.

“I was told you were killed in a boating accident while down in Cuba,” she said in a quick voice trying to hide her past indiscretions. “You’re alive?” she said as a question.

“Yes honey,” I replied. “But please don’t say anything to anyone. I’m being hunted by some really bad people, and if they find out I’m still alive, they’ll track me down and finish the job they started.”

“Wow, oh my God, that’s awesome Dad. I mean the part about you being alive. I’m so glad we didn’t lose you. After losing Mom, I’ve been totally lost, and I prayed you were still alive. My prayers have been answered,” she said in a feigned happy voice.

“Where are you staying now Teresa?” I asked. “Are you with Tonya, or have you moved out on your own?” I added.

“No, I’m living on my own in Washington D.C. I’m staying in a townhouse in Georgetown, with a boyfriend who is an older guy, but he has taken particularly good care of me,” she said.

“What’s his name?” I asked.

“You don’t know him Dad, and I’d like to keep it that way,” she responded. “But I’m doing fine and I’m so glad to hear you’re still alive,” she said.

“I’d like to apologize for storming out of the memorial service you had at your hacienda after Mom’s funeral. I had too much to drink, and the grief was just too much. I hope you’ll forgive me?” she asked.

“That’s not anything you need to apologize for baby,” I said. “I completely understand.

“You don’t know how someone could have found out our whereabouts in Cuba, do you?” I asked Teresa not sure how she would respond.

“No, not at all,” she answered. “I know it wasn’t me. I’d never do anything like that to you or Mom,” Teresa said in a crying voice.

“If I did that, it certainly wasn’t intentional,” she said. “I would never do anything to harm either you or Mom,” she repeated again, sobbing.

"It's okay baby. Just be careful when talking about me. Remember, you can't let anyone know I'm still alive," I said to her again.

"Where are you at now?" Teresa asked. "Are you still in Cuba?"

I wasn't sure I could trust her but decided to take the first move in rebuilding our relationship. "I'm in Virginia, at a farmhouse in Leesburg.

"I'm in hiding and will call you again when we can meet, maybe somewhere in Georgetown. I miss you so much," I continued.

"Wow, you're close," she responded. "Yes, I'd like that," Teresa added.

"Here's a cell number you can reach me on in an emergency, but I need you to promise you will not tell anyone about our conversation today," I reiterated.

After writing down my cell number, she hung up from the phone call she never expected to receive and immediately put a call into her boyfriend, Granger Adams.

"Hi baby," Granger said as he got up and closed the door to his office. "What up?"

"Jason Williams is alive and in the Washington D.C. area," she said to him in a panic voice.

"What! You must be mistaken," he said. "Your father died in Cuba. He was lost at sea somewhere, my sources told me. What makes you think he's still alive?" he asked.

"Because I just spoke to him," Teresa responded in a very worried tone. "He is alive, and he knows I told you where you could find him and my mother," she continued.

"I'm not sure why he is here, in the Washington D.C. area, but he wants to meet with me. I don't know what to do honey," Teresa said in a scared voice.

"It's okay baby," Granger replied. "Give me a little time to think things out, and we'll put together our next step. In the meantime, don't mention this to anyone," he said. "This needs to be our little secret for now."

Chapter 22 – Counter Move

The time had come. I ordered Dylan Rains to begin the negative social media blitz against *The Knights of Freedom*.

Dylan had identified a dozen or more servers that would control the distribution of the social media blitz. It began with several hundred social media sites being inundated with thousands of negative comments about *The Knights of Freedom*. This was a world-wide effort, and it included every country that allowed its people to have access to the internet and to the popular social media websites.

The file servers Dylan controlled were causing every negative posting to re-post repeatedly, making their message viral. The entire country and a good part of the world was now being made aware how bad the *KOF* really was, and what they really stood for.

The one item I chose not to make public, however, was the relationship between Granger Adams and the New Muslim World Order. This, I chose to hold back and use as my final weapon.

Granger Adams was not taking this sitting down. He wasn't sure who was behind these attacks, but now that he knew Jason Williams was not dead, he suspected Jason and Dylan Rains were involved somehow. He knew these two were out to destroy what he had worked so hard to establish. He knew if he were to succeed with his plan to establish a Union-of-States, he would need to eliminate these two adversaries. And he would need to do it quickly.

Granger's plan was to lure Jason Williams into Washington D.C., where he could set a trap to capture him and Dylan at the same time. He decided to use Bill McPherson, without his knowledge, and Teresa to accomplish this.

The plan began by summoning Teresa to the White House. When she arrived, he brought her into Bill's office, so she could meet the President.

"We need your help honey," Granger said to Teresa. He didn't want to make this a battle against the *KOF*, so he took a different approach with her.

Granger began the conversation with, "We understand and can only imagine how obsessed your father is with getting his hands on the CIA agent that tortured your mom, and we think we can help him do that.

"I put some feelers out and the CIA responded back to me with the name of their agent who did these devious deeds," he said. "He was told to not harm your mother, but apparently there was a darker side to this guy no one knew about," Granger told her.

"We want to make it up to your father for what happened, and I think by turning this agent over to him, it would go a long way to saying we're sorry. I think this would make him incredibly happy. Don't you agree?" Granger asked her.

"You know my Dad," she said as a matter of fact. "He's a vengeful and vindictive person. If he gets his hands on that agent, there'll be nothing left of him to return to the CIA," she said. "But I think my Dad would be very grateful to the both of you if you can give him that moment," she continued.

Not sure what Granger was planning, Bill jumped in and said to her, "Then that's what we'd like to do. If you know how to contact him, or the next time he contacts you, tell him we are glad to hear he is still alive, and let him know we have found out the name of the agent involved, and we're willing to arrange for your dad to have the opportunity to take his revenge out on this agent."

"His name, by the way, is Spider Webb, and we can put the two of them together," Granger jumped in. "We just need you to arrange the handoff. Can you do this for us?" he asked.

"Well, I have no way of contacting him, but if and when he calls again, I'll be sure to tell him about your offer," she said to the two leaders sitting in front of her. Granger stood up and put his arms over her shoulder and gave her a kiss on the forehead.

Teresa knew she had just lied to the President of the United States, but she wanted to keep her options open and play both sides of the fence.

Chapter 23 – Implementing the Plan

Although Samantha had returned to Gitmo after leaving the farmhouse in Leesburg, Virginia, she was not far from my mind.

During my first few weeks of recovery, I would talk about her to Douglas, and tell him how she cared for me on board the U.S.S. Tequesta. "She would bring me food and water several times a day and stayed around to make sure I ate the food and took the liquid," I told Douglas.

Realizing how important she was to his brother's recovery, Douglas arranged for her to immediately be transferred from Gitmo to the Marine base at Quantico Virginia. He felt she would be closer to Leesburg, should he need to get the two of them together. He knew I would need help both physically and mentally, and he knew she could play a major role in his recovery and well-being.

I stopped in my tracks when the burner phone I had been using sparingly began to ring. I saw it was not Teresa's phone number, so I wasn't sure whether to answer it or not.

Concerned no one knew I was alive, except for my inner circle, which included Teresa and Samantha, I decided to mask my voice and answer the call. I pressed the green button and said in a fake Spanish voice, "Hola."

"Jason, it's me, Samantha. You sound funny. Is it okay that I call you at this number?" she asked.

"Hi Sam," I responded in an exuberated and relieved voice. "Yes, no problem," I said, "but it's just a burner phone, so I don't know how long I'll have it. And yes, it's great to hear your voice again. Is everything alright?" I asked.

"Everything is fine Jason. I just missed you and was wondering how you were doing. I don't know if you've been made aware yet or not," she continued, "but I've just been transferred to the Marine Base in Quantico Virginia. Douglas had me relocated here in case he needs me to work with you some more. I think he likes the idea of you and I getting together," she said.

"I will be checking in at the Quantico base tonight, but I don't begin my duties at the base for a few days. I thought since I had some time, maybe I could come visit with you. Would that be okay?" she asked.

"Yes, I'd like that," I said without thinking. "It would be wonderful to talk with you again. There's a lot going on in my head, and hearing your voice, and talking about some of these things with you would be wonderful," I said in a surprisingly rapid voice.

"How's tomorrow?" she asked. "It's less than an hour drive to Leesburg from the base. I could meet you at the farmhouse, or we could meet halfway, say in Manassas, somewhere off route 234. That's only about half an hour from where you are. We can walk the old battlefield, and picnic somewhere out there, just the two of us."

"I think it's a bit chilly for a picnic," I responded, "but we could get some coffee downtown, near there. That's an out-of-the-way area, so I'm sure no one will spot me. I'll wear a hat and some dark glasses," I joked.

I keyed in some search information on my burner phone and then said to Samantha, "I'll meet you at the Starbucks on Galveston Court just outside of Manassas at noon. It's a secluded Starbucks, so hopefully, it'll be empty."

"That sounds terrific Jason, I'd love to see you again," she said.

Knowing I didn't want to give her the wrong impression, I said to her, "You should know I'm not ready to move on from Christine yet. I may never be ready to move on," I added.

"It's okay. I completely understand. I'm not looking to start up a formal relationship," Samantha said back to me. "I'm just looking to ensure your well-being and to help you make the transition from that hell hole at Gitmo, back to a normal life in the United States again."

"Then we'll just call it a consultation," I responded, "not a date."

Samantha laughed and said, "See you tomorrow at noon."

****

Dylan broke the silence, "We're ready Jason," he said. You just need to give me the word. My men are waiting for your order to execute the six key players in the *KOF*. The six who had a role in the abduction of Christine, and in your incarceration at Gitmo."

"Give me their names again?" I asked as I sat down at the kitchen table.

Dylan responded, "First is the woman who led the abduction of Christine. Her name is Traycia "Angel" Torres. She's the owner of the boat that attacked your hacienda and left with your wife. I was able to identify her by the tooth you found there.

"Second is the Captain of the ship, Benedict Warren. He was the captain of the ship during the time Christine was held captive.

"Third and fourth respectively are the CIA director who ordered the assault on your compound in Cuba, and the FBI director who jointly supported the efforts of the *KOF*. If they had not authorized this action, none of this would have occurred and Christine would be alive today," Dylan continued.

"And finally, there are two from the Senate Intelligence Community," Dylan continued. "Senator Kokingham from Minnesota and Senator Harold Rosen from Arizona. Both men are key to the success of *The Knights of Freedom*.

"All we need to do is get these laser rifles to my team, the United-Six, and they'll take out all of these bad guys simultaneously," Dylan said.

"Great job Dylan," I replied. "Okay, here's what I'd like to see happen," I said feeling back in charge.

"Since the Social Media blitz is working great, let's escalate our attack. Let's begin by shutting down their source of income. Close and lock their accounts permanently. This will let them know someone is attacking them, which will cause them to stop in their tracks to identify who this is. Remember, they don't know I'm alive," I added. "At least, I hope they don't know.

"Then initiate the final blast of negative social media posts that will totally discredit their organization. Add to the negative comments information about Granger Adams' new plantation in Georgia. The public needs to know he is a crook, and someone who is only looking to better himself, and not them," I continued.

"And don't forget their offshore bank accounts and their attitude toward women," I added. "Those offshore accounts need to be seized and the *KOF*'s feelings toward women needs to be exposed.

"This will be a wakeup call for Granger Adams as he begins to see his power crumbling before him. He won't know what hit him or who is pulling him under. Then we can set up the winds of change." I added.

"And what do you see as the final Winds of Change phase?" Douglas asked.

"I've got a pretty good idea how to end his tyranny and use what the ***KOF*** has created to bring the country back together again," I responded. "But first, I've got to talk with Bill McPherson and find out where he really stands in this battle. He is going to be key to undoing the damage that has already been done by the *KOF*."

"Dylan, go ahead and put your men in position," I continued, "and be ready to take down these six individuals when I give the order. You'll need time to get these weapons out of the farmhouse and in place at your various locations. And you'll need time for your men to learn how to use these laser rifles. I'd say, they'll have four to five days before they need to be in position and ready to shoot."

Dylan nodded his head, and said, "I agree. We will need prep time. Good thinking."

"Douglas," I said as I looked his way. "I think we need to bring Teresa in. We can't leave her with Granger Adams, once we begin physically assaulting him and his group. She'll be the first one he'll retaliate against,"

I looked at Douglas and asked, "Is this something you can take care of? You'll be putting yourself in harm's way, but we need to try and get her out of there before the fireworks start," I said knowing this could result in a second member of my family being killed.

"I'll take care of it," Douglas responded.

"Once Teresa is out of harm's way," I continued, "I will give Dylan the order to begin taking down the key players in *The*

Knights of Freedom. At first, I think we should begin with the two that had the closest contact with Christine and the easiest to take out. That would be the ship's captain and the skipper of the boat that took her. Then we'll follow up those two shootings with the two Senators on the Intelligence Committee, Kokingham from Minnesota and Rosen from Arizona."

Dylan jumped in, "Granger Adams will know right away the killing of these four was not coincidental. He'll know it's you and you're alive," he said looking at me.

"Once those four hits are made, I think it would be a good time to set up a meeting with Granger Adams," I said as I took a deep breath and let the air out with a sigh. Any disagreement?" I asked the two men at the table.

"Then there are only two decisions remaining," I added. "The first is what to do about those two at the White House, and the second is how do we get this guy called Spider Webb, the man who physically tortured Christine?"

Chapter 24 – Starbucks

It was 40 degrees outside with some wind and rain when Samantha arrived at the Starbucks about fifteen minutes early. But apparently not early enough to be there before me.

"Hi there," I said as she walked in the door. "I got here a little early also, to get a table in the corner. Hope this is okay?" I said as she made her way to the back corner table.

"It's perfect," she said as she smiled, taking off her winter jacket and sitting down across from me. "I'm ready for a good hot cup of coffee," she said as she turned and viewed the menu. "I think I'll have a Caramel Macchiato. How about you?"

"Sounds great, make it two. You'll have to pay as I don't have any cash or credit cards on me. The guys wouldn't give me any," I said to her.

A few minutes later, we were sitting alone in the corner, sipping our coffee, and laughing about how I looked.

"I almost didn't recognize you," she said. "You know you can take your raincoat and sunglasses off inside," she said as she laughed.

I smiled, then kind of laughed at myself, and said to her, "Are you sure?" as I removed my disguise. Looking more like a normal person, I asked, "So, how are things at Quantico?"

"Busy," she replied. "I was only back in Cuba less than a week when I received orders transferring me from Gitmo to Quantico. I had a lot of things to get in order before leaving the island," she replied. "But I'm glad to be gone."

"So, tell me how you and Dylan became so close," she said to me trying to get me to open up about my past.

"Wow, the interrogation continues," I said. "Well, I met Dylan when I was in Secret Service training at Quantico, Virginia," I began. "He is six years younger than me, and at that time, kind of on the wild side. Dylan lied about his age to get into the Secret Service and had a contact in personnel who faked his background check. He wasn't in his twenties yet, and that's the age they looked for in new recruits.

"I can say with certainty he wasn't a classroom kind of guy. After a short stint, he dropped out of the Secret Service training program and joined the Marines. He spent an enormous amount of time in the Middle East. That's where he lost his leg.

"I lost track of him for many years but heard he had become one of the best technology gurus America had. I'm told there isn't anything he can't hack into now," I continued. "I love the man and would do anything for him."

I smiled as I began to tell her the story of me and Dylan one night while still in Secret Service training. "We had been at this dingy bar one night, shooting pool and drinking beers, when after a few too many beers, some guy purposely bumped into me and decided I was the type he could easily kick the shit out of. He began to pick a fight with me and surprised me with a shove that caused me to land butt first on the floor. As I started to stand up, Dylan jumped in between us, pulled a knife from his foot holster, and held it over the left eye of this guy. He asked the guy if he really wanted to keep that eye.

"That caused the guy to urinate in his pants. He immediately apologized to the both of us, ran from the bar and the rest is history," I told her.

"Really," she said laughing. "I guess you're indebted to him then?" she asked.

"Yes, in more ways than one. He has always had my back. I think he feels indebted to me, but he's not.

"He's the one who saved Christine and my son from *The Knights of Freedom*'s bombing attempt on the Circle Cruise Line in New York several years ago. And he's the one who uncovered the *KOF*, and their plans to destroy this country as we know it," I continucd.

"So, he's a computer hacker?" she said.

"The best," I responded. "After Christine and I went into exile, he moved in with us at the hacienda. He wanted us to think he was protecting us, but I think he just didn't want to be alone. When Christine and I re-married, Dylan was our best man. At the wedding, he met a gorgeous Cuban lady and within a few weeks, he moved into town with her," I said as I looked up at Samantha.

"How about Anthony," she asked. "He is so much older than you. How did he become one of your loyal buddies?"

"You have a lot of questions, Sam," I said. "How about telling me a little about you?"

"Okay, you're right. I'll let you in on my life," she responded. "I'm from California, originally. Grew up in a redneck area just outside of Riverside, in a small town called Norco. It's about 70 miles east of Los Angeles," she began.

"I ran away from my parents' trailer at seventeen and moved in with a biker who was always drunk and very abusive. After my third trip to the hospital, I left him and joined the Marines. That was ten years ago, and I've never looked back," she said. "He never came looking for me, and that's a good thing.

"The Marines trained me to be a nurse. They also made me tough, and now at twenty-seven, there isn't anything I'm afraid of. Nothing," she repeated.

"How did you get to Gitmo?" I asked. "That's not exactly prime duty," I continued.

"While in nurse's training, I learned to speak

Arabic. That made me unbelievably valuable to our government, and they asked me if I would serve at Gitmo for a year. I did, but when my year was up, they begged me to stay on for one more year. They said I was a gifted nurse and a gifted interpreter. Especially when interrogating prisoners, they said."

"But as the world turns, I spent the last three years there. I'm glad to be out of that place. It can really screw with your mind. It's contrary to what you believe the United States stands for," she said.

"I do what I'm told, and I'm a good soldier, but still, it plays with your mind," she concluded as she looked up at me, who was staring at her with one of those caring looks.

The two of us talked for almost an hour. "Wow, I need to get back to the farmhouse before dark," I said. "I'd love to continue this consultation, but I really have to go," I told her not realizing how much time had passed.

"Well then, how about if we continue the consultation later this week. Say, the day after tomorrow?" she asked me.

"I really think these talks are therapeutic for you," she said. "Maybe we could take a walk through the battlefield next time?"

"I don't see any problem with that," I said, "as long as the weather cooperates."

"Okay then, noon at the battlefield the day after tomorrow," she replied as we got up and left the restaurant heading in opposite directions.

Chapter 25 – Turning up the Heat

I awoke the next morning with a smile on my face. I just spent the prior afternoon with someone who cared for me like Christine did. And I was beginning to get the same feeling toward her.

I immediately jumped up and out of bed and turned on the TV in the kitchen and stared as I saw something I hadn't seen in years. It was the word ALERT.

Then the caption at the bottom of the screen took my breath away. It read: ***The President has been shot.***

I turned up the volume and found myself standing in front of the television. I watched with intensity as the video they played brought back memories of 1962. It showed the President of the United States bent forward after being shot from behind, with Secret Service agents leaning over him from the back of his convertible. Only this time, they were tending to a slumped over Bill McPherson.

The TV reporter said there has been no word

on the condition of the President, and no word on a possible shooter. The TV reporter did say, however, there appeared to be no blood splatter in the car, and it may not have been a handgun or rifle shot that hit the President.

Another reporter indicated whatever the President was shot by, made no sound. And the President's clothing seemed to immediately begin to burn like something they've seen when lasers are used.

"Holy shit!" I thought. "Did Dylan act without first clearing this action with me?" I forgot about my coffee and immediately put a call into my long-time friend to find out if he had acted on his own.

"Hey," Dylan responded as he answered the phone. "Are you just getting up?" he asked. "If you haven't already done so, turn on your TV and take a look at what just happened," he yelled.

"I'm already watching it," I responded. "Was this you or one of your people?" I asked. "This is not what we had planned."

Dylan immediately responded with, "No, sir. It was not one of my folks. I wouldn't do anything without checking with you first," he assured me.

"Well, please drop what you're doing and put a full-throttle effort into finding out what's going on here. We need to know if the President is alive or dead. Something is not right, and we need to get more information before moving forward," I told Dylan.

"I'm already on it," he said and then hung up the phone to begin checking the internet for information. He knew some of the information he would find would be bogus, but he hoped the dark web would lead him to who might have done this, and how.

After a few hours of searching, he called me back. I was able to answer the phone on the last ring before it went to voicemail.

"Dylan," I said in a hurried voice. "What did you learn?"

"The first thing I was able to uncover was the President is alive and being treated at Walter Reed Medical Center. He is being treated for severe burns to the chest, not a gunshot wound," Dylan said.

"Burns!" I interrupted. "What's that all about?"

"Second, he was apparently shot with a ZKZM-700A Laser weapon exactly like the ones Koshi got for us," Dylan continued.

"Sounds like we're not the only ones with this secret hard-to-get weapon," I said. "How can that be?" I asked in a puzzled tone. "I thought we were the only ones with that weapon."

"So did I," Dylan responded. "So, I called your good friend Koshi.

"It appears the NSA informed Granger Adams about your purchase of these weapons from him. They conducted a surprise raid on his South Beach facility and threatened him with closing down all of his gun emporiums.

"They demanded he provide Granger with the same weapon he got for you." Dylan continued. "To prove they meant business, they shot Koshi in the kneecap, and now he's walking with a cane.

"Sergei is really distraught over this," Dylan added, "but was told by Granger Adams if he leaked a word of this to anyone, it would be the last gun he ever sold in the United States."

"Are you telling me you think Granger Adams put the hit in on the President of the United States and is trying to make it look like I did it as some sort of revenge shooting?" I asked Dylan.

"I don't think he tried to kill the President, but yep, I think that's exactly what happened," Dylan responded. "But we can make this work in our favor," he said.

"Yes, I see where you're going with this," I responded. "Once we put out proof Granger Adams shot the President of the United States, he will be the one that is hunted, and hopefully jailed. This, plus all the negative information we've already put out on the ***KOF*** should bring him down," I continued.

"But this means he already knows I'm alive and here in the United States," I added. "The only way he could know this, is from Teresa. We need to bring her in now," I said as a final thought.

"Go ahead Dylan and release your men to hit the first four targets on our list," I instructed Dylan. "Taking out the Senators will put the fear of God in the others in our government that are supporting Granger. If they think they might be next, we might be able to weaken his support. And maybe they'll think it's Granger who is shooting at them."

Chapter 26 – Getting Teresa

I placed a call to Douglas to find out where he stood with regard to getting Teresa out of the grasp of her apparent boyfriend. Douglas answered the phone, "Can I call you back in five minutes Jason?" he said.

"Please do," was my response.

It was probably twenty minutes later before my burner phone rang, and I heard the voice of my brother on the other end. "Jason, it's me, don't hang up," Douglas said.

"Hey," I responded. "Are you're okay? This situation is getting worse by the minute. I believe Granger knows I'm alive. I think Teresa ratted me out," I said.

"Well, it wouldn't be the first time," Douglas mumbled, and immediately regretted those words.

"What the hell does that mean?" I asked.

"Not now," he responded. "We can talk about that later. Right now, I'm heading over to Granger's townhouse to hopefully find Teresa there. If she's there, I'm going to take her away. Forcibly if I must. This entire situation is about to blow up, and if she's in the middle of this, she'll become a casualty. Hopefully, she'll listen to what I tell her, and she'll come willingly," he said.

"You need to make sure this happens," I said quite firmly to my brother. "I gave Dylan the go-ahead to begin his first round of hits. They should occur sometime tonight or tomorrow.

"And, I'll be calling Granger tonight, to try and set up a meeting with him for later in the week. If you see him, plant a seed that you think he should think about some sort of meeting with me. Tell him, talking with me is in all of our best interests," I continued.

"Okay, I'm in Georgetown now and will be pulling into Granger's townhouse driveway in a moment. I'll call you back when I have Teresa," Douglas said as he hung up the phone.

After knocking for several moments and ringing the doorbell twice, the door finally opened. Teresa was shocked to see Douglas there and wondered how he knew about her and Granger. "What are you doing here?" she said with a smile as if she was a kid caught with a handful of candy.

"Teresa, we need to talk, and we need to do it quickly," Douglas said as he gave her a welcoming hug. "Can you come with me for a drink, so we won't be worried your boyfriend comes back while I'm here?" he asked her.

"I understand," she responded. "Is everything okay? Is my dad okay?" she continued. "We both know he's alive and in Virginia somewhere."

"Your dad is fine, for now," Douglas said. "But I don't want to talk here. Can we go?" he said urgently.

"Sure, let me get my purse and I'll be right with you," she said as she ran back inside for a quick moment. Douglas watched her as she ran back to the kitchen. He wanted to make sure she didn't try to call anyone.

To his surprise, she just got her purse and within a minute or two, they both were heading down Wisconsin Avenue and over the bridge into Arlington. They pulled into a favorite restaurant of his called The Sushi Garden. It was a quiet place where they could just talk.

Douglas ordered two Grey Goose martinis, straight up. He knew he needed to get Teresa to calm down, so she could think through what he was about to tell her.

When the waiter returned with their drinks, Douglas said to him that they just wanted to talk for a while before ordering. The waiter understood and left them alone.

"Teresa," Douglas began. "You know we all love you and we are one hundred percent behind whatever it is you want to do with your life. The only purpose for my visit now is to make sure you are safe from what is about to happen to everyone you know," he said in a soft tone while holding his hand on top of hers.

"You are the daughter of one of the most hunted men in this country. And yes, he has screwed up his family priorities a few times in the past, but that has changed," Douglas began.

"When he was able to reconnect with your mom, everything changed for him. He was able to see what a fool he had become. I know you have your doubts about what I'm saying, but just know he genuinely loves you. He loves all three of his children more than anything," Douglas continued.

Several minutes passed as they both downed their martinis. Douglas signaled the waiter for two more, and they arrived within moments.

"Uncle Doug," Teresa said removing her hand from under his. "He always told us that we make our own bed, and that we have to sleep in it, or something like that," she said. "Well, he made his bed when he left mom," she said.

"Teresa, Jason didn't leave your mom. Your mom told him she wanted a divorce, and she asked him to leave. He loved her."

"Well, he loved being a cowboy, out to save the world, more than he loved us or her," Teresa responded back. "I want to be happy, and right now I'm happy being with Granger. I know he and Dad are at odds, but in time, they'll get over it. Especially if I marry Granger," she said surprising Douglas. "I would hope Dad would come to the wedding, and we'd all be happy," she said.

"Teresa, none of what you think is going to happen will happen. Granger Adams is the second most powerful man in this country.

And he has made plans to create a smaller country within our borders and become the President of that country. Once that occurs, he's gone," Douglas said.

"He's only with you because you are a link to Jason, the one man that can bring his quest to an end," Douglas told her.

"He is using you to keep tabs on his hated enemy," Douglas continued. "Granger has already arranged to relocate his life to Tennessee, and it doesn't include you," he told her. "He's returning to his roots in the south and will become the head of the new confederate statehood known as the United Southern States of America.

"Our country, as we know it, will become divided in two, with two Presidents, two governments and two ways of life. Is that what you want to become part of?" he asked her.

As Teresa began to tear up, Douglas again took her hand and put it in his. He softly said to her, "Within the next few days, beginning as early as tomorrow morning, both men will openly and physically attack each other.

"There will be many casualties, and your dad has sent me here to make sure you're not caught in the crossfire. All hell will break loose, and the last thing he wants is for you to get hurt, or worse yet, killed."

"Killed!" she said. "Are people going to be shooting at each other?

"Is this why you're here? To tell me I must choose between Granger, who I think loves me, or my dad who I know doesn't love me? If that's the case, it's an easy decision," she continued.

"Okay, I didn't want this conversation to go this far, but it looks like it must," Douglas said to her.

"I want you to know about the man you think loves you," Douglas continued.

"He is the man responsible for your mother's death. When you told him where in Cuba your dad was hiding, he sent an extraction team in to bring him back to the United States to stand trial for treason.

"When they didn't find your dad home, they kidnapped your mother, and brought her to a perverted CIA interrogator who mutilated and raped your mom and left her to drown on a sinking ship. All that on the orders of the man you think loves you," Douglas told her.

"You couldn't be more wrong about him," Douglas said as he chugged down the rest of his second martini. "We're talking about your mother. The woman who gave birth to you," he said.

Teresa now crying, asked Douglas what he wants her to do.

"You need to come with me, right now. No going back to the townhouse, no phone calls, just leave with me, now. I'm going to take you to my place until we can find a safe location for you. It's the official house of the Vice President, although I only stay there when I must."

"But I don't even have a toothbrush or a change of clothes," Teresa said.

"That'll all be taken care of," Douglas assured her.

"Okay," she reluctantly said. "Can we eat first?" she asked. "I'm starving."

Douglas smiled and called the waiter over, so they can order some sushi and a couple more martinis. Once done, they headed back over the bridge and up to the Vice President's mansion in Georgetown. Douglas put a quick call into me to let me know he had Teresa and they can begin counter activities.

After hanging up the phone with my brother, I sat down with a glass of bourbon, took a sip, and put in a call to my arch-enemy, Granger Adams.

I assumed Granger did not recognize the caller-id on his personal cell phone since he let it go to voicemail. Anticipating this, I left a prepared message. "It is in our best interest to talk," I said point blank. "I will call you back tomorrow, at this exact time, to set up a meeting agreeable to the both of us." With that, I hung up the phone.

Chapter 27 – A Walk in the Park

It was another blustery morning, as I pulled into the huge parking lot at the main entrance to the Manassas National Battlefield Park. I walked over to the Henry Hill Visitor Center and spotted Samantha who was waiting for me.

I snuck up behind her and as I approached, cupped my two hands over her eyes. "Guess who," I said in a deep voice.

"Is it my husband?" she said as she broke out into a full laugh she couldn't contain. As she turned around, she said, "The look on your face is priceless. Your jaw was hung down, and you had this sad look in his eyes."

"I'm only kidding Jason. I'm not married," she said as she pulled me closer and gave me a giant hug. I liked that, and as she hugged me, we began to laugh at the joke.

"Wow," I said. "I really need to lighten up." Seeing that we were hugging, we both let loose of each other and backed away as if we had done something wrong.

"You made it," I said with a giant smile.

"Yes, I did," Samantha responded. "I've never been here before. Have you?" she asked.

"Nope, first time for me," I said.

We picked up a map of the battlefield inside the visitor's center and began our trek out around the cannons and statues. "It's nice to be out here with you Jason," she said. "A bit chilly, but nice.

"Do you mind if we continue to talk about you and your friends?" she asked.

"No, not at all," I responded. "Just don't take advantage of me. I'm still feeling vulnerable, and I may get emotional if you hit close to home," I said with a smile.

"You were telling me about your interaction with your close friend, the President of the United States, Bill McPherson. How was it being that close to a President?" she asked.

"Bill and I were friends," I began. "I'm not sure if we still are friends with everything that's been happening lately. So, it wasn't like I was with this person of high stature. It was just Bill and me. When he needed me, I made sure I was there for him. When I needed him, he was there for me," I explained to Samantha. "That's what true friends are all about."

"And now that you think he's supporting this subversive group that you are against," she asked, "are you guys still friends?"

"We're going to find out soon," I responded. "We're going to find out soon," I repeated as I examined one of the many cannons located in the park.

Samantha shook as a cold gust of wind kicked up. I quickly walked over and put my arms around her, to try and keep her warm. She liked that, and easily nestled into my arms.

We spent hours touring the battlefield and holding hands. I did most of the talking, as I was slowly becoming the man I used to be. I was becoming more comfortable with myself.

Chapter 28 – Negotiation

The morning sun was bright as I lay there in bed. I had just spent the last two hours thinking about the questions Samantha asked me at the Battlefield yesterday. And I had also been thinking about what my relationship with her was all about. Was it something I really wanted to pursue? Was I dragging her down into the gutter I was wallowing in? Did she deserve that, I wondered?

I knew Dylan would be calling soon to let me know how his men did. Were all four of the planned hits successful?

And I knew later tonight, I'd have to set up a meeting with Granger Adams. I was glad I hadn't mentioned Granger Adams' name to Samantha. The less she knew, the better off she'd be, I thought.

My burner phone rang, and I recognized the number. It was not Samantha and it was not Teresa. It was Bill McPherson. He's probably calling from a hospital somewhere thinking that I had tried to kill him, I thought to myself.

"Hello Bill," I answered in a good-ole-buddy voice. "Good to hear you're alive and well," I said.

"Really?" responded Bill. "I'm not sure if I can believe that. I'm told you put the hit out on me. Is that true?" he asked point blank.

"There is no way I would ever put a hit out on you," I responded. "I may have my differences with you, mostly because of your support for *The Knights of Freedom*, but I would never try to kill you," I added. "At least not yet."

"Then why was it I was burned by one of your laser guns?" Bill asked. "I'm told only you had these special weapons."

"Not true Bill," I said. "I guess Granger didn't tell you he used the NSA to track down the gun dealer who sold me those weapons and acquired an exact duplicate for himself.

"And why do you suppose he did that Bill?" I rhetorically continued. "So, he could shoot people and make it look like I was responsible.

"If you're looking for the person who tried to

have you eliminated from the picture, look no further than your buddy Granger Adams," I said to Bill in a raised tone of voice.

"I'll have my people check into that with the NSA, and if I confirm what you say is true, I'll have him arrested.

"If you're lying to me, then I will truly be saddened to know someone who I spent most of my life with, and trusting them, would try to have me assassinated," Bill said with a sad tone in his voice.

"Bill," I responded, "Granger is setting us both up. He's hoping to drive a wedge between the loyalty you and I have. I want you to know I did not try to have you assassinated, and if I were to plan something like that, I'd personally do it myself, right in front of you," I told Bill.

"That's how I would expect you to do it." Bill hesitated as he said that. "What can I do to help?" he asked me. "Do you want me to have him arrested?"

"No, I don't. Not just yet. I'd like you to say nothing and give no indication you're beginning to question Granger. I want him to think everything is still as it was and he has you in his back pocket. When the time comes, I will ask you to show your true loyalty, and it will be to our country, not to me or Granger Adams," I said.

Again, I chose not to mention Granger Adams' relationship with the New Muslim World Order.

While on the phone with Bill, my other burner phone rang. This time it was Dylan Rains. "Gotta go," I said to Bill McPherson as I hung up with him and answered the phone call from Dylan.

"Jason," Dylan shouted out. "It's not public knowledge yet, but I just heard the ship's captain, Benedict Warren, was found dead in southern Cuba. He was apparently shot with one of those laser rifles, like the one used to shoot the president."

Dylan continued, "And they say his body was found next to an American woman named Traycia Angel Torres. She was the leader of the group that picked up Christine. I told you about her.

"I'm guessing Granger was eliminating anyone who could lead us back to him, while tying you to these murders. The word on the street now is Jason Williams has gone crazy and is now planning to kill everyone associated with the kidnapping and death of his wife.

"In response to these killings, Granger has arranged for you to be added to the FBI's ten most wanted list."

"That means I cannot go out in public," I said. "It may change how we move forward."

"Well, you are officially a fugitive now," Dylan said. "It's hard to believe, but Granger Adams is constantly one step ahead of us. We need to turn the direction of the tide, or we'll not succeed in our plan," Dylan said with a sigh.

"Okay," I replied in a pissed off voice. "I will lay low until I can set up a meeting between Granger and myself.

"I'll plan to meet with him and offer him a deal. We need to get him to temper his current plans," I told Dylan. "And you need to take charge of this situation," I continued.

"I'm counting on you and your men to keep Granger off my back. I will be calling him tonight, and I think we'll be able to make him an offer he can't refuse. I just need to think what that might be," I said as we ended the phone call.

It was around 5:45 P.M. and the sun had just set. This wasn't like the Caribbean. The sun sets early in the wintertime up north. I was punching in the phone number of Granger Adams, when suddenly, my phone started to ring. It was Dylan Rains again.

"Yes Dylan," I said with an annoying tone as I answered the phone. "I was just getting ready to call Granger Adams," I added. "What's up?"

"You better hold off calling that bastard. I think you need to sit down because what I'm going to tell you will really upset you to no end," Dylan said.

"Tell me," I shouted in a mad voice.

"Granger Adams has just been shot, and it's another laser rifle attempt," Dylan responded.

"Like the others, it was a serious assassination attempt, but I'm hearing the laser beam only burnt his shoulder. It burnt a hole clean through it, but they're saying he should recover."

Dylan continued, "So now, there is an aggressive manhunt out for you. Not only is the FBI actively looking for you, but so is the CIA, the DIA, and every local law enforcement agency in the Washington D.C. area. It won't be long before your location is uncovered and then you'll be incarcerated again. I don't know if you can take that," Dylan said. "We need to get you out of here, quickly."

"Are you telling me Granger had one of his own people shoot him, so he could blame it on me?" I said, not believing my own words.

"That is exactly what happened," Dylan responded. "So now he's got you shooting the President of the United States and the Speaker of the House," Dylan said.

I thought for a moment and then said to Dylan, "Hold off shooting the two Senators from the Senate Intelligence Committee. I can't have two more bodies added to my acts of vengeance."

"Yes," Dylan said, "I agree. I'll pull my guys back from that one temporarily," he continued.

"Okay, I need to talk with Granger Adams," I

said. "I'm going to call him right now and see if I can get him to call off his dogs, and to see if there is some type of deal we can make that will end this madness."

A few minutes later, I heard those words I had been longing to hear for months.

"Hello Jason," the voice on the receiving end of my phone call said. "Your smear campaign on the internet is not destroying my reputation. The American public don't care what we do, and they're not going to believe your lies, so you need to stop filling the airways with this bullshit and misinformation," Granger said in a pissed-off tone.

"They are believing the word out on the internet," I responded. "And as for bullshit and misinformation, I don't know what you're talking about, Granger," I said. "It's all true."

"You know exactly what I'm talking about," Granger said in an angered voice. "You know you're a wanted man, don't you Jason," he continued, "by every law enforcement agency in this country? I'll have you back in Gitmo before the sun comes up tomorrow," he added with a smirk.

"Granger," I responded. "You are a smart man. I'm sure you know your plan to frame me for these recent murders, and for shooting you as well, will not work. I've already put the word out on the street that blames you for these shootings. And I'm sure you now know you've pissed off the Cuban drug cartel by killing the daughter of its leader Ronaldo Torres. I hear he's looking for you right now, so watch your back, my friend," I said with a pause.

"And for your ridiculous plan of getting the states to ratify the creation of your new Union-of-States, that will not work either. Not as you hope it will. You know the rest of the country will revolt against you, and you will not see your dream come true of being the President of anything."

I paused but didn't hear a word back from the other end of the phone call. "But" I said in a consoling voice, "I have an offer I think you're going to like," I continued.

"I'm listening," Granger replied.

"What if I can assure you the presidency of the current United States of America?" I said.

"I don't think you have that kind of power,"

Granger snarled back.

“What if I provided you with an irrevocable written order by Bill McPherson that would guarantee your appointment?” I said.

“What kind of written order,” Granger asked, “would give me that kind of leverage?”

“How about multiple photographs of our current President, Bill McPherson, having sex with two underage girls?” I responded. “If I had Bill prepare an order that both he and Douglas Williams would resign their positions as President and Vice President, you would automatically become the President of the United States as third in line.”

“You have photographs like that?” Granger asked.

“Yes, I do,” I responded. “And I can make all this happen. You know my reputation.”

“I’m still listening,” Granger replied.

“These photos can be yours if you’re willing to trade for something I want just as bad,” I continued.

“I bet I know what it is you want,” Granger said back to me.

"I'll bet you do," I responded back. "I want the man that tortured my wife onboard the ship she was held captive," I said. "I want Spider Webb turned over to me."

"I don't think you're in a very good position to be telling me what you want," Granger said. "What I will do, however, is call off the dogs that are hunting you for forty-eight hours, while I think about all you've said. That will give you time to think about my counteroffer to you," Granger continued.

"And what counteroffer is that?" I asked.

"If you call off your plans to try and terminate *The Knights of Freedom*, then I will let you live. And I will let your family live as well," ho said. "Othcrwioc, you'rc all dead."

"So, we both have something to think about," I responded.

"Yes, we do. Call me back in forty-eight hours and we'll continue this conversation," Granger said as he laughed to himself and hung up the phone.

Chapter 29 – Visit with Teresa

It was early evening when I fell asleep, probably around 8:00 P.M., only to awake a couple of hours later, screaming and trying to grab the snakes I imagined were covering my body as I slept.

This was a recurring nightmare I couldn't shake. In bed only a couple of hours and already my body was soaked and the sheets I lay on were soaked as well.

Now almost 10:00 P.M., I decided to call my brother Douglas, and ask if he could bring Teresa out to see me in the morning.

"Douglas," I said as the phone call was answered immediately on the first ring. "It's me, Jason," I said. "How are you, and how is my daughter?" I asked.

"We're all fine," Douglas responded. "We're just sitting here catching up on each other's lives. I must say, Teresa has been around the block a few times. She's a pretty smart girl. Kind of a chip off the old block," Douglas said with a laugh.

"Can you bring Teresa here tomorrow?" I asked.

"Do you think that's wise, considering the farmhouse could be attacked at any time," Douglas responded.

"It should be okay," I said. "I spoke with Granger Adams a few hours ago, and he has agreed to call off the dogs for forty-eight hours while he considers an offer I made to him," I continued.

"Do you think it's a good idea to bring Teresa there?" Douglas asked again. "Maybe we could just meet somewhere in the middle. That'll give you a chance to talk with her and to assess whether she's truly gone to the dark side, or if she will side with us," Douglas continued as he knew Teresa was listening to his every word.

"No, bring her here please," I responded. "I want her to know I trust her, and I'm willing to expose myself one more time, to prove it. However, to be safe, bring her to the large farmhouse down the hill."

"Okay, we'll be there around nine in the morning," he said. "Is that okay with you?"

"Perfect," I said.

Before heading to the guest bedroom, I decided to send a text message to Tonya and to Justin. It read, "I would like to have a 2:00 P.M. EST conference call tomorrow with all of my children. Teresa will be with me. We need to begin bringing our family back together again. Are you in?" the message read.

It was almost 11:00 P.M. when my burner phone received the two replies I was hoping to get back. "Yes," from Justin and "Yes" from Tonya, the texts read.

****

The sun was shining through the window of the guest bedroom, directly onto my face, causing me to open squint my eyes closed. An hour later, after dressing and downing a quick cup of coffee, I headed down the hill to the second farmhouse Anthony had purchased for us.

This farmhouse was an emergency safe house and an old trick of the mafia back in the day. When they purchased hideaways, they always acquired two of them. One was always backup to the other, should it be needed. And this time, it was about to get a tryout.

I was about to receive a visit from Douglas and from my daughter who I hadn't seen since Christine's funeral in Santiago de Cuba almost six months ago. I settled in, put my backpack in the master bedroom, and made the house look like someone was living in it.

Thirty minutes after arriving there, a government SUV pulled into the driveway, followed by three Secret Service vehicles. Two people exited the front SUV, Teresa from the passenger side and Douglas from the driver's side. No one exited the three other vehicles. They just remained there in case they were needed.

I met my brother and my daughter on the front porch, which wrapped around the house providing a full view of the twenty-one acres that came with the house.

"Wow," Teresa said. "Is this yours?" she asked as she stepped up to meet me on the front porch.

"It could be ours," I said. "Anthony acquired this for us, and if things go the way I hope they do, we could make it ours."

"How are you Dad?" she then inquired as she gave me a timid hug. "I heard you spent some time locked away at Gitmo," she added. "You look good, and Douglas said you were doing fine. Just a few nightmares now and then," she said as she laughed.

"Well, it's good we can laugh about it now. But it was pure hell when it was happening. Luckily, Dylan was able to come to my rescue," I responded.

"It was great talking with you the other day. I really missed you," I said as I gave Teresa a big hug in return.

"Come on in you two," I said as I opened the screen door and pointed toward the kitchen. "I've got breakfast cooking on the stove, and coffee brewing by the sink."

Teresa and I talked for hours as I tried to explain my actions over the past dozen years. I did what I did for love of my country, I told her. "I had a loyalty to Bill McPherson, as you know, and he asked me to work on his campaign. I guess I could have said no, but you guys were always running here or there so I figured you wouldn't mind if I abandoned you for a year or so," I said to her.

"I can understand what you're saying, but Mom needed you there, and you weren't," she said back to me.

"Well, your Mom and I made up, and we moved on," I said. "That's why she agreed to go to Cuba with me. That's why she married me again. We had a chance for a re-do and we took it. We were incredibly happy together until it all ended abruptly. I'm not holding anything against you personally, but I am holding your boyfriend responsible," I told her.

"Yes, I know you are living with Granger Adams now," I continued. "And that's your call. You're a grown woman and are free to make your own decisions. I just want you to be safe because I am going to take him down. And when I do, there may be collateral damage."

"I understand," Teresa said. "I've got a lot to think about, and I will not betray your trust. I think we've all been through enough, and it is time to bring our family back together again," she said.

I couldn't believe what I was hearing. "Yes, I agree," I said. "Last night, I texted your brother and your sister and told them we'd do a conference call this afternoon. I hope this can be the first step to reconciliation. We need to not look backward. We need to look forward," I told her.

After breakfast, Douglas said, "I'll clean up. You two go check out the farmhouse and the property. It'll give you two some alone time. The morning is beautiful, just a little chilly, so go explore," he said.

"Sounds great," I responded. "Let me get one thing from my bag and I'll be ready to go," I said.

I came out from the master bedroom carrying a police stun gun Dylan had gotten for me. "Here, hang on to this Teresa," I told her. "If we're out there alone, we may need to use it."

We walked out onto the front porch and took a deep breath of the fresh air that permeated the farmland. We jumped into one of the two gas-powered golf carts that was stored in the barn and rode off to explore.

The breeze was cool and the air clean. Each hill we rode up exposed another hill. The property was majestic, and the white-railed fence that lined the property was a beautiful contrast to the green fields that lay before us. Up and down, we rode, talking and laughing. I was at peace with myself, and with Teresa.

It was almost 2 P.M. when we returned to the farmhouse.

"Wow, where did you two go?" Douglas asked. "I thought maybe you guys ran away or something."

"This place is gorgeous," Teresa said. "The property is huge, and we could build several houses on it, and still not be right near each other. And we're only a forty-five-minute drive to downtown Washington D.C.," she noted. "I really hope we can get the family back together again," she said.

As planned, I made a call on my cell phone to Tonya and Justin. For the first time in many months, the four of us talked together. The event was warm, cordial, and exactly what I wanted.

After the call was over, Douglas and Teresa headed back to Washington, to the Vice President's home. Before leaving, Teresa gave her father a big warm hug. It was something I had not felt in years.

On the way back to Washington, Douglas asked Teresa if she were going to stay at his home for a while until her father gets things squared away with her boyfriend?

"I'd like to, I think," she answered. "It looks like there's room for me," she laughed.

Douglas laughed also. "My place has thirty-three rooms which should be enough for you and me. Did you get to see the pool out back?" he asked. "It's heated, you know. And don't forget the house is also home to the atomic clock, so you'll never be late for anything," he said as they both laughed.

"And then once things are settled, it would be nice to live out on that farm in Leesburg," she said.

As they drove back along route 7, back toward Reston, the sprawling hills and farms all looked so beautiful. Even the pop-up suburbs that dotted their route all had beautiful entranceways. This was horse country, and it was beautiful.

Chapter 30 – Farmhouse Raid

Douglas pulled into the driveway at One Observatory Circle, dropped Teresa off, and told her he'd be back later tonight. "I have several obligations I must attend to at the White House, so you're on your own for the rest of the evening," he said as he pulled back out into the street.

Within twenty minutes of being dropped off at the Vice President's home, Teresa was in a cab and headed back to her boyfriend Granger Adam's townhouse.

"Hey baby, where have you been?" Granger asked her as she walked in and he put his arms around her and hugged her tightly. "I missed you last night, and all of today as well," he said as he kissed her on the neck a second time.

"I was with my dad," she said, causing Granger to step back and stare in amazement at her with wide open eyes.

"Your dad," he repeated back. "Where did you go to see your dad?" he asked.

"Leesburg," she replied. "He's staying at a farmhouse off Loyalty Road. And it's beautiful," she said in an excited tone.

"Wow, that's a surprise," he said back to her.

"Granger," she looked up at him and asked, "are you planning on leaving Washington, to go live down in Tennessee somewhere?"

"Wow." Granger again stunned, asked, "Is that what your father told you, honey? Well, it's not true," he said to her. "I'm staying right here, hopefully with you baby," he responded. "Isn't that what you want?" he asked.

"Yes, it is," she replied to him as she headed upstairs to shower and slip into something more comfortable. "I'll be down in about an hour," she said running up the stairs.

Granger immediately dialed Garrett Johnson and told him Jason is staying at a farmhouse in Leesburg, on Loyalty Road. "Take care of it now," he said to Garrett.

Within minutes, a local squadron of police, along with the ATF to ensure the Federal Government could take me away on weapons charges, swarmed the farmhouse Teresa and I were at only hours earlier.

I sat in the kitchen, which looked down the hill to the farmhouse on Loyalty Road. I watched as a dozen cars pulled up, with red and blue lights flashing. Using my burner phone, I videotaped the entire raid on the farmhouse below.

I recorded as they busted down the door and ran inside with weapons drawn. I continued videotaping as they came back out, and as one of the ATF officers made a phone call obviously reporting back that there was no one there.

"Douglas was right," I thought to myself. "She could not be trusted. At least not yet."

The call from the ATF commander to Garrett Johnson did not go well. The local police department wanted answers. They told Garrett they were not taking responsibility for breaking into a house obviously no one lived in. They wanted to know who was going to repair the damage to the property they caused?

"We'll take care of it," Garrett assured the police officer on the other end of the line.

Garrett then called Granger Adams and told him what the result of their raid netted. "Absolutely nothing," Garrett said.

"Whoever told you Jason was there, was lying," Garrett said in a pissed-off tone. "Now I've got tracks to cover and paperwork to follow up on. Get it together Granger," Garrett said.

Granger had two glasses of wine poured and was sitting by the couch when Teresa came downstairs. He raised his glass as she entered the room, and she quickly joined him on the couch.

"So, tell me about your visit with your dad," he said.

"Well, there's not a lot to tell. We spent most of the day touring the farmhouse he purchased now that he's back in the country. We're hoping to reunite the family, and possibly build some homes out there on this huge farm. It's over twenty-one acres according to my dad," she continued.

"And it's on a street called Loyalty Road?" he asked.

"Yep, his brother picked me up and took me there," she said.

"Well, I hope you enjoyed your time with him," Granger said. "I'll be talking with him tonight, and hopefully we can put past anger aside, and all become family," he said to her as he leaned in and gave her a warm kiss.

Granger was almost three times her age and found her company boring, but she did turn him on. She was pretty, but not the brightest star in the sky. "Glad I won't be dragging her around much longer," he thought to himself.

It was obvious to him her father had tested her loyalty, and she had failed. He had set her up, by taking her to a farmhouse he obviously wasn't staying at, to see if she'd turn on him. And she obviously did.

It's ironic the street he had her brought to was named Loyalty Road. "I'm sure this issue will come up in tonight's conversation with her dad," he said to himself.

"Honey, I've got to leave for a while. I need to prepare for that especially important phone call I'll be receiving soon. I'll come up to bed when I return. Okay?" he said as kind of a question to her.

"Yep," she replied. "I'll be upstairs when you get back."

While upstairs, she received a video text from me, showing the raid on the farmhouse she was at earlier this morning. On the screen were the words "don't trust him."

Chapter 31 – The O-Lounge

It was well after midnight when the alarm on my cell phone went off. I quietly got dressed, threw on a jacket to hide my Beretta, and tiptoed down the steps into the living room. Dylan was fast asleep in one of the downstairs bedrooms, so I had to be careful not to make any noise.

As I quietly snuck outside, I walked down to the bottom of the hill where I had left my rental car. I turned the key one position to the right and put the car into neutral. I then pushed it down the slight hill until I was clear of the house and could safely start up the engine without being heard. Within seconds, I was away from the house and heading down route 7 toward Washington D.C.

I arrived at the O-Lounge around 1:00 A.M. This was a strip club in Tysons Corner, Virginia that stayed open until 4:00 A.M. As I walked in, sitting in the corner was the man I came to meet. I walked over to where the man was sitting and slid into the booth.

A sultry looking waitress approached and before she got too close, I said to her in a raised voice, “JD on the rocks, double.” She nodded and was back in a few minutes with my $15 drink.

Forgetting I had no cash, I pointed to Garrett Johnson, Bill McPherson’s Chief-of-Staff, and said, “Just put it on his tab.”

“Glad you were able to make it Jason,” Garrett said in a soft voice.

“I’m taking a big chance being out in public, and in meeting you here like this,” I said as I sipped my JD on the rocks. “So, let’s be quick and let’s be brief,” I continued.

“You got my cell number from Teresa and sent me a text saying we need to end this conflict between Granger Adams and myself and you could help. So, I’m here and I’m all ears.

“What is your plan?” I asked as I leaned more toward the center of the table.

“Jason,” Garrett began. “I am on your side. I am not your enemy. I love this country and I am loyal to Bill McPherson who is a friend to both of us,” he continued. “I would take a bullet for Bill, and I know you would also. We're on the same side," he reiterated.

"Unfortunately, the Speaker, Mr. Adams, has gone off the deep end," Garrett continued, "and is literally running amuck. He is going in a direction the President and I don't want to be heading down," he said. "He has resorted to activities that are unacceptable to us.

"He has decided that he will do whatever is necessary, be it legal or not, to establish the United Southern States of America. That is unacceptable to me, and to our organization, *The Knights of Freedom*."

"So, what did you expect?" I asked. "The man is a bigot and a racist, and he isn't much interested in what America stands for. He is an old guard southerner and has his own personal agenda. And the good of the country is not on his list."

"I am aware of that, and so are my friends who want to help you take him down," Garrett said.

"I am glad to hear you see this for what it is," I said. "I am willing to do whatever is necessary to remove Granger Adams from the head of your organization. And I can use all the help I can get," I responded.

"But it will cost you," I added. "My price is the handing over of your CIA Interrogator, Spider Webb."

I knew I had made a similar offer to Granger Adams, but I didn't know if that offer would be accepted, so this was just an insurance offer. "If you can do that," I continued, "then we can work together on this one goal," I said as I lifted my glass as a toast to what I hoped would be an agreement.

"I can meet your requirement," Garrett said, "but I must insist *The Knights of Freedom* be allowed to continue after Granger Adams is removed from its leadership."

"That is something I cannot agree to," I interrupted. "This country will not survive having eleven states secede from the United States. I am going to continue with our plan to keep that from happening. There can only be one United States of America," I reaffirmed.

Garrett shook his head in disbelief. "No, that cannot happen," he said. "When Granger Adams is removed as head of the *KOF*, I will step in and assume the vacant leadership position," Garrett said clearly.

"And why is that?" I asked.

"Because too many side agreements have been made by Granger Adams, and they each need to be dismantled. We're talking about agreements and plans with foreign countries that will consider any failure on our part to honor those agreements and plans a violation of world protocol and an act of war.

"If I cannot redirect the *KOF*'s plans," Garrett continued, "then I will do as you say and close it down. This is a huge organization, with worldwide influence, and they will need someone leading it that is influential within our government."

"What plans?" I asked.

"Are you sure you're ready for this?" Garrett said with a laugh. "Granger Adams has agreed to set up a new state, a Muslim state to be precise, in exchange for the support of almost ten million Muslims throughout the United States. He is asking this group, that has grown tenfold in the last few years, to rally their congressmen and women to support the constitutional amendments up for ratification. If the amendments pass from the states with high Muslim populations, he promised them their own State in the new Union of States, with their own laws."

"Their own State? You have got to be kidding me," I said in disbelief.

Garrett continued, "That's why I said he went off the deep end and needs to be stopped. What he has promised cannot be allowed to exist. Not within this country," Garrett said.

"Members of *The Knights of Freedom* who are just hearing about this, are not accepting this plan, and neither should we," he said looking directly into my eyes.

"We need Granger Adams dead," Garrett said in a slow but forceful tone.

"Who are you working with?" I asked. "You said we."

"There is an exceptionally large and important ally who wants in on the Oil Trifecta Bill McPherson now heads up. They hope by helping to derail the *KOF*, they will be rewarded with entry into this group. They are hoping a vacancy will occur because of the alliances made with the NMWO," Garrett responded.

"A vacancy?" I repeated the words. "By whom?"

"By Saudi Arabia," Garrett replied. "They have failed to keep the lid on the terrorists in their own backyard and have lost the confidence of our President. And the ones I'm trying to help will move into that vacant spot. You know who they are," Garrett continued.

"The ones you are working with?" I repeated as a question. "Who is that?"

"They were the ones who made you aware that the explosion on board the Emerald Green was an inside job," Garrett responded.

"Okay, I get it, but why do you need me to do this?" I asked. "You certainly have plenty of organizations within the government that can take care of this."

"Yes, we do, but I need the world to know this was the result of action Jason Williams took. It can't be thought of as an inside job, by power-hungry politicians. It must be a vengeful act by a grieving husband who evened the score on the man who was responsible for the death of his wife.

"When all is said and done, you won't have to worry about being charged with a crime. It will all go down as part of your effort to bring down *The Knights of Freedom*. And I'm sure in time, you will be victorious in your effort and all will be forgiven," Garrett said. "If you're found guilty of anything, POTUS will surely pardon you as quickly as possible," Garrett said.

"So, do I understand you to say you think the *KOF* will be successful in their attempt to create a Union-of-States in the south?" I asked, not expecting an answer.

"Yes, I do," Garrett answered to my surprise. "I know that's surprising coming from me, but it's what I think will be the outcome from all this. I think Granger could end up creating his Union-of-States, and he will be forced to deliver on his agreement with Assam Bashula," Garrett said. "And when it does all come to fruition, I think it will all eventually fall apart, and the country will suffer from what he did. That's why I need him eliminated," Garrett continued.

"Well, this is not what I expected to hear come from your mouth Garrett," I responded. "I will take your request seriously and see what I can arrange. I will call you later today and advise you of my decision. "

It was well after 2:00 A.M. when I left the O-Lounge and headed back to Leesburg.

I arrived back at the farmhouse to find Dylan sitting at the kitchen table, waiting for me.

"Fuck, where have you been?" Dylan shouted jumping to his feet as I entered the farmhouse. "I have been worried sick you were kidnapped or something."

"I'm sorry Dylan, I didn't want you to worry. That's why I didn't tell you I was leaving or where I was going," I responded.

"Sit down and I'll fill you in. Then I need to get some sleep because tomorrow, I mean later today, will be a busy day," I said as I sat down next to Dylan at the kitchen table.

"I just met with Garrett Johnson, Bill's Chief-of-Staff," I began. "Garrett is orchestrating a power-play for the leadership of *The Knights of Freedom*, and he wants me to terminate Granger Adams. He is willing to hand over

Spider Webb to me once this is done, but that's not the issue anymore. The issue is do we assassinate the Speaker-of-the-House?"

"Well, isn't that our goal?" asked Dylan. "You want the *KOF* to be gone and getting rid of its leader should definitely accomplish our goal."

"It goes deeper than that," I continued. "Garrett is colluding with the Russians on this.

"They are looking to get in on the Oil Trifecta that Bill heads up and want to ensure this country is not split in two. They are afraid if this happens, control of the world's oil could possibly end up in Venezuela, and that's the last thing they want. There is apparently a private take-over of Venezuelan oil fields underway, by private owners, and this could shift the balance of power further away from the Russians."

"I am aware of that," Dylan said, "and I agree. This is bigger than originally thought."

"And to make matters worse," I added, "Granger has made deals with several foreign countries, including Syria, if they help him receive the ratification votes he needs to get his southern states to secede.

"But killing the Speaker-of-the-House. I don't know?" I said as a question.

"Maybe we can use Ronaldo Torres to help us with this dilemma. After all, Granger killed his one and only daughter," Dylan suggested.

Chapter 32 – Let's Make a Deal #1

Granger Adams answered the phone within seconds of its first ring. He was obviously waiting for the call and had a detailed script in front of him of his demands and his concessions.

"Hello Jason. I hope you're enjoying the nice cool weather here in the nation's capital?" he continued with an I don't give-a-shit attitude.

"I am," I responded with the same tone as the pleasantry was sent.

"Good, I'm glad to hear it," Granger countered.

He took a moment to compose himself and then got right to the point with me. "I've given your offer a great deal of thought and I'm willing to move forward," he said in a willing-to-work-together tone. "Do you have the photos in your possession?" Granger asked.

"I do," I responded. "But let's just work on the first step in our agreement which is for you to turn Spider Webb over to me," I continued. "You do that, and I'll hand over clear and incriminating evidence that will get you into the Oval Office."

"And a signed statement from the President, that Douglas Williams will also step down when POTUS resigns," Granger asked. "Do you have that as well?" Granger asked.

"Yes, I have that as well," I responded, knowing this was a lie.

"Then, agreed," Granger said firmly. "I can arrange to turn Spider over tomorrow night, at midnight, in the North Plaza parking garage, on the 3rd floor, at the John F. Kennedy Performing Arts Center just off Rock Creek Parkway. Do you know where that is?" he asked.

"Yes, I do, and that's perfect," I said. "There's plenty of cover there and the place should be fairly empty. But, no more than three of your people should be there, along with your friend, Spider. I'll limit my men to a total of three also," he said. "That way, no funny business will occur."

"Let's just make it me and your daughter Teresa in my vehicle. I'll bring Spider Webb, so you'll need someone to watch him once you leave. You bring Dylan Rains with you and that's it," Granger countered. "That way, I know it'll be safe for both of us. I know you wouldn't try anything funny if there was a chance your daughter could get hurt," Granger continued

"Agreed," I responded. "See you at midnight, tomorrow night," I said to Granger as we hung up the phone.

Chapter 33 – Granger Changes the Rules

Granger Adams didn't get to be the head of *The Knights of Freedom* because he trusted people.

He became head of that organization by taking control of situations, and by not leaving anything to chance.

Immediately after ending his phone call with me, he was on the phone to Garrett Johnson.

"Garrett, I want to have that lieutenant lady, Samantha something or other, here tomorrow morning. You know, the one Douglas just transferred to Quantico," Granger ordered.

"She's going to be key in our plans of capturing Jason," he continued. "Tell her, she's not to mention this to anyone and don't tell her who she will be meeting with. If she refuses to come, have her commanding officer order her to attend this meeting. He can tell her she's attending on my request," Granger said to Garrett Johnson.

"No problem, I'll have her there," he told Granger.

After hearing what Granger Adams told him about their plan to meet with Jason Williams and exchange Spider Webb, Garrett felt this might all be part of Jason Williams' plan to kill Granger Adams. Although he never did get a confirmation call back from Jason, he assumed Jason had accepted his offer.

At 0600 the next morning, MP's at Quantico entered the duty office of Lieutenant Samantha Wilkinson, who had just begun her watch two hours earlier.

She was informed her presence was immediately required on Capitol Hill for a highly classified meeting of national security. Within a few minutes of the MP's arrival, she was on her way in the President's personal SUV, for the ride back to Washington D.C.

One hour after traveling on an empty I-95, with flashing lights and sirens blaring, her escort arrived at the White House. She was quickly taken to the President's Chief-of-Staff, Garrett Johnson's office.

The young lady that just arrived at his office, was going to be bait, along with Teresa, for the big fish they hoped to catch. After a few pleasantries and a quick tour of the Oval Office, Samantha and Garrett made their way over to Granger Adams' office on Capitol Hill. Coffee and donuts greeted their arrival.

Samantha was in awe of everything she'd seen at both the White House and on Capitol Hill. In her entire career, she had never been inside either of these two buildings.

"Miss Wilkinson," Granger said in a soft voice. "I apologize for whisking you away from your duties at the base so early this morning, but it is important you be here now."

"We have a very important, high-level national security meeting," Granger continued, "that we need you to attend with us later tonight. We need you to interpret exactly what is said from some Iranian agent we are meeting with.

"The meeting will be held in a parking garage at the Kennedy Performing Arts Center, and it involves obtaining the release of six American hostages being held by the Iranians. We need you to let us know if he is being truthful in what he says. It's more of an assessment of his tone, not necessarily his exact words. Can you do this for us?" Granger asked her.

"Yes sir," she responded, "I'd be happy too, but I don't understand why it is me you've selected for this assignment. Don't you have interpreters here at the White House?" she asked.

"Well yes, but Douglas has talked so highly of you, we thought it would be a good opportunity to get you vetted for future assignments," Granger told her.

"We've reserved a room for you at the Watergate for the afternoon and early evening and we'll plan to pick you up around 11:30 P.M. That way you can review your Arabic in the meantime and get some rest before we head out. It's going to be a long night," Garrett said to her.

"Oh, and one more thing Samantha," Granger said to her. "You cannot tell anyone you are here. If word gets out I'm bringing someone to this meeting, other than the ones the Iranians have approved, the meeting will be called off. Do you understand?" he asked.

She nodded in the affirmative and was taken to the Watergate Hotel on Wisconsin Avenue.

Chapter 34– The Exchange

At precisely 11:30 P.M., Garrett picked up Samantha from the Watergate Hotel. He escorted her to Granger's Chevy Suburban and helped her into the vehicle. He then headed to the second SUV and climbed into the front passenger seat.

As Samantha peered into the back, she saw a woman sitting back there she had never met. Also, in the back seat was a man she did not recognize either. He was bound and gagged and was sitting next to the woman.

"Hi," the woman said, "I'm Jason Williams' daughter, Teresa. And you are?" she asked Samantha.

"Lieutenant Wilkinson," she responded. "U.S. Marine Corp." Samantha was confused but decided to remain quiet.

The two Suburbans sped off and in a few short minutes, turned off Rock Creek Parkway and into the north plaza indoor parking garage. Garrett's SUV parked on the first floor, while Granger's vehicle made its way to the third level. Upon arriving, they found Jason's vehicle waiting for them.

Parked face-to-face, we both signaled with our headlights that everything was a go. Granger stepped out of his vehicle, arm still in a sling from the laser wound he sustained the other day, and pulled his male hostage from the back seat leaving the two women alone inside. He walked halfway to where Jason was standing, dragging the man Jason Williams came to collect.

I looked at Spider Webb with madness in my eyes. The overweight man in front of me was shorter and heavier than I thought, but for sure, he was nasty looking. I walked over to him and spit in his face.

"Hold on Jason," Granger said. "He's not yours yet. I need to see the photographs you have," he said.

I opened my briefcase and handed Granger the photos. Then I handed him a signed affidavit from Bill McPherson that stated he would resign, along with his Vice President, Douglas Williams, clearing the path for Granger Adams to become President of the United States.

"These documents will all but assure that you will be appointed President of the United States of America when both men resign," I said.

As Granger was looking over the photos, Garrett's government Suburban vehicle pulled up onto the third floor of the parking garage and barreled toward the three men standing there. The vehicle stopped about twenty feet away from us, but no one emerged.

As Garret's Suburban came to a stop, I looked through the front windshield saw Samantha sitting there, along with my daughter Teresa who was in the back seat.

At that same moment, Dylan Rains jumped out of the passenger side of my SUV and pointed a weapon at Granger.

"Hold on hot-shot," Granger yelled at Dylan. "They are my assurance I get out of here alive. No one will get hurt if we all remain calm."

At that same moment, three of Garrett's men emerged and surrounded me. One of the gunmen slammed the back of his rifle into the back of my head, causing me to fall to the ground. The men picked me up and put me, along with Spider Webb, into Granger's SUV.

Dylan fired his weapon at Granger, hitting him in the leg. Moving behind his SUV for protection, Dylan fired at Granger again, but missed.

Granger limped back to his vehicle and climbed in behind the wheel.

Teresa seeing what they had done to her father, decided she had had enough of this guy and removed the stun gun she had gotten from her farmhouse visit and pressed the button as she slammed it into the back of Granger's head.

She fired and Granger's head jolted forward into the steering wheel. The impact dazed him enough that Samantha, reacting from instinct, pushed him out of the vehicle and onto the garage floor.

Within half-a-second, as Granger picked himself up from the cement floor, he grabbed Teresa from the back seat and pulled her out of his vehicle. In obvious pain, Granger pulled out his Glock and pressed it against Teresa's back. Without hesitation he pulled the trigger and let my daughter Teresa, fall to the ground.

Garrett thought for a second and considered taking out Granger Adams now. With all the confusion, no one would know he took the shot that killed the leader of the *KOF*.

However, he regained his composure and decided to let things play out. He really wanted Jason to be blamed for killing the Speaker-of-the-House.

Stunned and enraged by what had just happenned, I jumped out of Granger's SUV and ran toward Teresa.

Dylan, with his rifle aimed at Granger, yelled to me, "Pick up Teresa and put her in the back seat of our SUV now."

I did as Dylan requested, and then hopped into the back seat alongside the bleeding body of my daughter.

Dylan, who was in complete command of the situation, held Granger at bay and walked over to the Speaker's SUV and grabbed Spider Webb, pulling him from Granger's vehicle. He then pushed Spider Webb into the back seat of their SUV where I was sitting. Samantha immediately jumped out of Granger's vehicle and climbed into the driver's seat of Dylan's SUV.

I held Teresa in my arms, and not thinking, yelled to Samantha to get us the hell out of there. Samantha, believing everyone was loaded into the SUV, slammed her foot to the floorboard and drove across the third floor of the garage and down the ramp.

Spider's hands were zip-tied behind his back, so I pushed him down onto the back floor. My foot rested on the back of Spider's neck.

I leaned forward and instructed Samantha to drive to George Washington University Hospital up on 23rd Street. "It's just up the road less than five minutes from here," I said.

"You'll have to take her in, and stay with her," I said. "I'm still a fugitive, and they'll arrest me. You can tell them you found her lying in the street. I'll head back to the farmhouse and you can call me with any updates."

Samantha confirmed the plan as she drove north toward 23rd street, following the signs with the big "H" on it. Samantha asked, "What was all that about? And what about your friend Dylan? We left him there," she said.

"Dylan knows how to take care of himself," I responded. "We'll be able to better help him from the farmhouse than from the streets of D.C.," I said as my cargo who was crunched on the floor of the back seat began to moan.

I held Teresa in my arms as we made the almost five-minute drive to the hospital. When we arrived at the hospital emergency entrance, I carried Teresa through the front doors and handed her to several attendants who came out with a stretcher.

Samantha went in with Teresa, running alongside the gurney, as I jumped back into the SUV. I was full of Teresa's blood, and my hands were wet on the steering wheel.

I hoped I wouldn't be stopped by Highway Patrol as I'd have a tough time explaining all the blood and my prisoner on the back-seat floorboard.

Chapter 35 – The Capture

Dylan, who was still in the garage, realized he was drastically outnumbered. He looked around but didn't see much of an opportunity to escape his situation.

Granger limped toward Dylan, who now had his arms held high in the air. "You are my prisoner now, my friend. If you want to get out of this alive, you'll need to drop your weapon and kick it over to me."

Dylan took a moment and decided to live and fight another day rather than die in a vacant garage somewhere in Washington D.C. He dropped his weapon, kicked it over to where Granger was standing and walked out from behind the SUV, his hands held high. "You win," he said.

In the background, he saw Garrett Johnson standing alongside one of the SUV's. He was directing the cleanup of the mess that was just made. Dylan looked directly into the eyes of the only person he felt could help him now, but Garrett looked away and pretended not to want to help Granger's new prisoner.

Granger, still bleeding from the gunshot wound he sustained from Dylan, drove his vehicle from the Kennedy Center into the garage of his Georgetown townhouse. His remaining bodyguards followed but stayed on the driveway.

One of the bodyguards got out and pulled Dylan from Granger's vehicle and escorted him down into the garage where he shackled him to wall brackets behind where the cars parked.

Then he pulled out a syringe and pushed it down into Dylan's neck. Dylan collapsed to the ground and was out within five seconds.

Chapter 36 – The Bad News

Several hours after arriving at the hospital, Samantha called and gave me the news.

"I just talked with the head of the surgical unit here at George Washington University Hospital," Samantha said, "and he told me Teresa didn't make it. She had lost a lot of blood, and the bullet was so close to her heart that it caused too much damage. I am so sorry Jason," she said as she teared up.

"God damn it," I said as I slammed the cell phone to the ground. In a fit of rage, I swung at everything in the room knocking lamps and pictures to the floor. Realizing Samantha was still on the phone, I sought out the cell phone I threw, picked it back up and said into it, "Are you still there?"

"Yes baby, I'm still here. Try to be cool. Let's get through this together, and it'll be alright," she said. "I assume they're going to need information from you regarding insurance and final arrangements, so will you give them a call?" Samantha asked.

"Yes, yes, no problem," I replied. "Tell them I'll call them later with all the details," I said as I began to tear up.

"Samantha, I need you. Can you get back here to the farmhouse? I'd come pick you up, but I don't think I'd be safe on the road in my condition."

"You know I want to Jason, but I must get back to the base," she replied. "They're sending a military vehicle to pick me up and take me back to Quantico. Once I get checked back in, I'll call you.

"The head of the surgical department told me since her death was caused by a gunshot wound, the police will need to be involved, and they'll want to talk to all of us who were witnesses to this shooting," Samantha continued.

"I don't know if you want all that to happen, so you've got some thinking to do. Let's talk in the morning, and see what needs to be done then," she said. "Right now, I need to get going."

"Thanks for being there for me Samantha," I said. "I'll have a better idea of what the plan is in the morning. Call me as early as you can."

The next morning, I sat alone, trying to think what I needed to do next. As I sipped my morning coffee, the call came in from Samantha. I answered it on the first ring.

"Hi Sam," I said as a smile came to my face. "Are things all good at the base?" I asked.

"Yes, Jason. Apparently, everything has been taken care of already. Your brother Douglas was able to pull a lot of strings.

"He called the base commander earlier this morning, and they have arranged for me to take a one-week leave of absence," she continued. "Tomorrow morning, they are also providing me with transportation to the hospital to pick up Teresa's body and bring her to a funeral home near the farmhouse in Leesburg. The head of the surgical unit will meet me there and assist with preparing her for the journey," Samantha replied.

Chapter 37 – Let's Make a Deal #2

I realized I had to deal with the issue of Dylan not making it back to the farmhouse. I also knew I would need to resolve the situation between myself and Granger Adams.

It didn't take long for my cell phone to ring. "Hello Granger," I said. "You are a dead man for killing my daughter, and I will do everything in my power to make you pay for that."

"Just makes us even," Granger said. "You killed Jennifer, who was someone I loved, so I killed someone you loved.

"The killing of your wife Christine was not at my hands", Granger continued. "I'm told she was collateral damage from an interrogator who took his work a little too seriously."

"You're fucking crazy in the head, Granger Adams," I responded. "And you better not hurt a hair on Dylan's head," I continued as I raised the level of my voice. "I want him back, and I want him back now."

"Hold on Jason," Granger interrupted. "I hold all the cards here. I want you, not Dylan," he said. "I am willing to swap your friend Dylan Rains for you," he continued.

"It's a deal," I replied. "You name the time and the location, and I will trade my life for his. But it'll have to be on my terms," I added. "I'm through trusting you," I said.

"Before we continue with any trade, I'll need proof you really have my friend in captivity. And I'll need proof he is still alive," I added.

"You shall have your proof, my friend. I will send you proof that I have him and that he is alive. Look for a package to be delivered when the sun comes up, and then call me back with a plan that will exchange him for you," he demanded.

"And if all this doesn't happen within the next forty-eight hours, then I will hang your friend and send you the videotape of his death."

As I hung up the phone, Douglas pulled into the driveway. His security unit waited outside as he came into the kitchen where I was sitting.

"Sit down Douglas," I said as he walked into the kitchen. "They've got Dylan."

"What?" Douglas said in a shocked voice. "What does that mean, they've got Dylan?" he asked.

"It means, Granger Adams captured Dylan last night at the Kennedy Center garage, and he's going to dispose of him in forty-eight hours unless I turn myself over to him, in exchange for Dylan," I said.

"Hold on Jason," Douglas responded. "We're not trading anyone."

"I need to save my friend and I need to act quickly," I shouted.

"Presuming Granger really has him, I need to be ready with an exchange plan," I said.

"Well, we should begin by sending a message to his team, the United-Six, and let them know he is in trouble. Let's plan to have them meet us here at the farmhouse tomorrow afternoon," Douglas said.

Within a few minutes of that suggestion, I texted Rachel who was the United-Six team leader and told her what had happened to

Dylan. I requested her presence at the farmhouse tomorrow at 2 PM.

Chapter 38 – Pulling Strings

It was 8:45 A.M. the next morning when Samantha's vehicle pulled up into the driveway of the farmhouse.

Reclined in the passenger seat was my daughter, Teresa, looking weak and without a lot of color, but alive.

Fearing the NSA would be listening in to conversations from the hospital, Douglas had arranged with the hospital CEO and the head of the surgical unit to fake Teresa's death, so she would be safe going forward.

No one knew of the plan, not even Samantha. It wasn't until Samantha arrived back at the hospital to pick up Teresa's body, that she was let in on the deception.

I couldn't believe what I was seeing. Douglas and I ran out and helped get Teresa up to the house. Samantha's driver carried in her two suitcases, along with a bag containing Teresa's old clothes.

"Good job Samantha," I said. "We can't thank you enough for helping sneak her out of the hospital and for bringing her here.

"Will you be able to stay for a while, to help tend to her needs?" I asked.

"Not a problem," Samantha responded. "Your brother was able to pull more strings and arrange a week's leave of absence for me, so yes, I'll be able to help take care of her."

"I'm sorry," Douglas explained. "I didn't tell you before they got here Jason. I just wanted to make sure everything went well getting her out of the hospital and getting her here. I felt it was in her best interests to not say a word."

"I'll need a room downstairs next to her room so I can be there if she calls out," Samantha said. "Can that be arranged also?"

"You bet," I responded. "I'll move a bed into my den, and you can stay there, right next to the guest room."

Samantha sought out the kitchen and then made Teresa some tea. She brought it in and pulled a handful of pills from Teresa's travel bag. "This should help ease the pain,"

Samantha said as she handed Teresa the pills.

"Oh, by the way," Samantha said, looking at me. "There's a box out on the front porch for you. It looked like it was from FedEx," she said.

I ran to the front door, opened it, and retrieved the oblong box which seemed to measure about eight inches wide and twenty-four inches long. Inside the box was Dylan Rains' artificial leg, along with a thumb drive.

"Oh my God," I said as I stood up and carried the metal leg and the thumb drive to my desk. I inserted the drive into my laptop, which automatically opened a file that showed Dylan Rains, alive, sitting in a chair at an empty table without his leg.

"That's Granger's kitchen," a weak Teresa said as she looked into my den at the laptop screen.

"Okay, that's where they're holding him," I said as I recomposed myself, and looked over to Douglas. "When Rachel gets here, we'll review the layout and the location of Granger's townhouse and put together a rescue plan."

"In the meantime," Samantha said. "I'd like for Teresa to get some sleep. The trip here had to be exhausting for her, and she's still in a pretty delicate condition," she continued. As they all left the room, Teresa sipped some of the tea and fell sound asleep within minutes.

We all reconvened in the kitchen. "Teresa sustained a serious gunshot wound to the chest," Samantha said. "The doctors said she needs lots of bed rest.

"I will tend to her needs," Samantha continued, "but what she doesn't need is aggravation or worry while she's here. I think she should sleep and eat as often as she can. That means you guys will have to help me prepare her meals and help with her medications. Are you two up for that?"

"Whatever it takes," I said to Samantha. "I know how helpful you can be, and I'm sure Teresa will be a good patient."

At that moment, Rachel Lynch walked in. She didn't knock, and no one heard her approach the farmhouse.

"You guys need to enhance your security here," Rachel said as she raised her right leg over top of the kitchen chair and sat herself down. “If we’re going to mount an assault rescue of Dylan Rains, we’re going to need to be able to protect him once we get him back here. And, what you have in place for security now, just won’t hack it,” she added.

“Now, has anyone been able to substantiate Dylan has really been captured and he is still alive?” Rachel asked.

I pulled out the box that contained Dylan’s metal leg, and I opened my laptop, so she could see Dylan sitting at a kitchen table in Granger Adams’ townhouse.

Chapter 39 – A Fawn in the Grass

It was 10:00 P.M. when things quieted down. Douglas, Rachel, and Rachel's Commander Jason Ramsburg, who joined Rachel at the farmhouse, had gone down to the lower farmhouse and turned in for the night.

I silently walked into the guest room where Teresa was sleeping. She was being watched over by Samantha. "How is she doing?" I asked, hoping to hear good words.

"She's doing remarkedly well, considering she took a close-range bullet to within an inch of her heart. That shot from Granger was intended to kill her. Luckily, she flinched just before he fired, or she would be dead by now," Samantha responded.

I walked over and looked down at Teresa, lying there like a fawn in the grass. She looked so innocent and pretty. "I could never hate her," I thought to myself.

Samantha was sitting on the side of the bed, as I leaned down and kissed Teresa's forehead.

As I moved upwards from that kiss, my eyes met Samantha's and for a moment, we looked deep into each other's eyes. I then straightened up and walked to a chair near the window in which I sat down and stared at Samantha.

"You are incredible, you know," I said as I looked at her. "You stayed by my side onboard that Navy ship, during my hours of need, and now you're by my daughter's side in her hours-of-need."

"It's what I do," she replied. "I'm a nurse."

"Well, you made me feel better," I responded. "I know I have not truly thanked you for all you've done for me and for Teresa. I hope you'll give me the chance to do that?" I said.

"I will," she responded. "I really like you and I like being with you," she continued.

Samantha stood up and walked over to where I was sitting and held out her hand to me. "I understand what you've been through, and I understand why you did what you did," she said holding my hands in hers. "Let's not spoil things with actions we're really not ready for. When the time is right, we'll know it," she said as she smiled at me and leaned in to give me a kiss on the lips.

I returned her kiss as I put my hands gently on either side of her face, pulling her toward me. For a moment, I felt happy, and I felt comfortable being with Samantha.

As she backed away and left the room, I smiled down at Teresa and felt love. I wanted to take away her pain, and all the traumas she had endured over the years because of me.

The next morning, Samantha had gotten Teresa out of bed and slowly walked her to the kitchen table. She sat Teresa down next to her father and her uncle. Samantha then joined us at the table.

"What a family," Samantha said to break the ice. "I am honored to be sitting here with you all," she said as she smiled.

Teresa drank some tea, downed half an English muffin, and asked to be taken back to bed. "This was great," Teresa said, "but I need to get horizontal again before I pass out. I'm getting stronger, but I don't want too overdo it."

Samantha got Teresa's wheelchair, so she wouldn't have to walk, and wheeled her back to the guest room, helping her get back into bed.

"Thank you, Samantha," Teresa said looking up and smiling as she spoke. "I remember you told me who you were when we were driving to the garage in Granger's SUV, but we really haven't been formally introduced," she said.

"Well, I'm U.S. Marine 2nd Lieutenant Samantha Wilkinson," she replied. "I escorted your dad back from Gitmo after Dylan and Rachel rescued him. He needed someone to care for him, just like you're needing someone to care for you," Samantha responded.

"Well, you are a special person," Teresa said in a weak voice. "I hear you brought me to the hospital after I was shot, and you stayed there with me during my surgeries. And you brought me here after getting them to release me earlier than they wanted to," she said as she squeezed Samantha's hand.

"It's what I do," Samantha replied. "As I'm sure you've noticed, I have grown to have some feelings for this family and I hope that won't be a problem with you," she added.

"I am the wrong one to talk about feelings," Teresa answered. "I've made a mess of all my feelings around people and am not sure anymore of what I should feel or think."

"It's okay Teresa," Samantha interrupted. "There is no game plan on feelings. We just make our decisions, and we go forward based on them. I'm a true believer thing will all work out in the end," she continued.

Teresa fell back and was asleep within minutes. Samantha covered her with blankets and a smile. As she did, she didn't notice I was standing in the doorway, observing her, and listening to her words. I wondered if that applied to me as well and whether things would work out in the end for me.

With that, Douglas, Rachel, and Rachel's Commander, Jason Ramsburg, came up from the lower farmhouse and entered the room.

"How's she doing?" Rachel asked.

"Coming along," Samantha responded.

"Good, then let's get a plan going here to get Dylan back," she said in military fashion.

Chapter 40 – A Moment of Trust

It wasn't until the third day of Teresa's recovery that I was able to feel comfortable my daughter would recover.

Although she had slept most of the two full days she had been there, I could see color coming back into her face. She was weak but stronger than when she first arrived.

With a plan in place, Rachel and her Commander Jason Ramsburg left the farmhouse that morning, along with Douglas. They were going to take up positions at the Vice President's official home. This would give them time to scout out Granger's townhouse for a raid to free Dylan Rains. It was his third day of captivity and they were anxious to get him back.

I called Granger Adams that morning to let him know I was willing to make the trade. However, Granger told me he's changed his mind and he has decided to hold on to Dylan. "I'll let you know when I'm ready to trade," Granger said and then hung up the phone.

I immediately put a call into Rachel and let her know what had just transpired.

"Looks like we're going to have to go in," she said. "I'll keep you in the loop, once we get Granger's townhouse scoped out."

Justin arrived in a rental car at the farmhouse around midday. He had been summoned by me to take over responsibility for caring for his sister. This would give Samantha a much-needed break as she needed to return to the base in a couple of days.

Since the lower cabin was now empty, I took Samantha aside and told her she looked like she could use an evening of rest and relaxation and she should plan to spend the night down at the lower farmhouse after she finishes putting Teresa to bed for the evening. I wanted her to have time to go over everything with Justin.

I told her I was going down to the larger farmhouse later to prepare an easy but fancy dinner for her, with a nice bottle of wine, some candlelight, and a warm bubble bath. I told her once I had everything prepared, I would leave her alone to relax and unwind, but that I'd be just up the hill if she needed anything.

Samantha was impressed with my concern and agreed to the arrangement. It was just past eight o'clock when she arrived at the farmhouse at the bottom of the hill. I had been there for a few hours, preparing a small cheese fondue for her, with a side of chocolate fondue for dessert.

I had drawn a bubble bath and placed a wine glass and an open bottle of red wine on the table alongside the bath. To sweeten her mood, he turned on some soft music in the background.

Samantha was impressed with what she saw. She was also impressed with the amount of trouble I went through in my quest to create a soft relaxing mood for her.

"Wow," she said as she entered the lower farmhouse's main living room. "You really know how to treat a woman. I am so exhausted, and I really appreciate what you're doing," she said. Did you mention something about a bath?" she asked.

"Yes, there is a warm bath drawn upstairs for you, with an expensive bottle of Kathryn Hall

Cabernet Sauvignon to help you relax," I responded.

"And when you've finished with your bath," I continued, "there is a small cheese fondue in the kitchen keeping warm for whenever you're ready. I also took the liberty of preparing some chocolate fondue if you'd like something sweet after dinner. I'm going to leave you here, alone, where no one will bother you," I added.

"Oh, and the master bedroom has clean linens, so you can spend the night there," I said as I headed to the kitchen.

"Breakfast will be waiting for you when you return to the main house up the hill, or whenever you wake up," I told her.

Samantha was in shock. "This all sounds so great. Thank you so very much for caring about me," she said as she walked into the kitchen and popped a piece of broken bread into the cheese fondue, and then into her mouth. "Hmmm, this is awesome," she said looking back at me watching her.

I didn't wait for any further thanks. I just quietly left her alone and walked back up the hill to the main house.

About forty-five minutes later, my cell phone rang, and I saw it was Samantha's number on my screen. I quickly answered it by saying "Room service. How may I help you?"

Samantha laughed and said she needed someone to wash her back and would I be interested in doing this for her? I laughed and asked how she was enjoying her alone time.

"Well, come down here and I'll tell you exactly what I think," she said as she laughed.

"Seriously, I just want someone to share the wine with," she said in a soft voice. "We can talk for a little while and then I'll turn in for the night," she continued.

Within five minutes, Jason knocked on the door of the farmhouse down the hill and walked in saying, "It's me. Okay to come in?"

Samantha was still in the bubble bath I had drawn for her. I didn't know whether to leave or just wait for her downstairs in the living room, but when I heard her say, "Hey, come in here and sit with me, I won't bite," it made me feel a little awkward, but happy.

"Are you sure?" I responded back to her in a semi-loud voice.

"Please," she said. "I'm so relaxed that nothing will happen between us. I just want to look into your eyes and thank you for being so caring."

I proceeded upstairs and entered the bathroom where Samantha was covered from head to toe in white bubbles. She popped her head up at the far end of the bathtub and smiled at me.

I sat in a makeup chair across from the bathtub and she could see I was trembling a little. She didn't want me to feel uncomfortable, so she said, "It's okay Jason, I'm just a person who thinks you're awesome. I won't pressure you to do anything you don't want to do."

"How about joining me for dinner?" she asked me in hopes of getting me to relax. "You made such a beautiful fondue, and I can't eat it all myself. Please?" she added as a question.

"Okay, you win," I said. "I'll meet you downstairs when you're ready," I continued as I stood up and left the room.

I went downstairs and began to plate some fondue. When I turned around, Samantha was standing behind me, soaking wet, with just a towel around her. I looked at her all wrapped up, put my plate of food down and leaned into her. I kissed her softly at first and then as our passion rose, I kissed her with more fervor.

She returned the passion and before we knew it, our hands were all over each other as the towel slid to the floor.

I lifted her up and carried her up to the bedroom where I fell onto the bed with her in my arms. We continued to kiss. Samantha pulled my shirt up over my head and kissed my firm chest. She worked her way down to my abs which were just as firm and hard. This raised the level of my passion to a height I hadn't felt in many months.

As Samantha climbed on top of me, her somewhat wet and soapy body was still gleaming from her bath. Her hair fell from the top of her head onto my shoulders. She was beautiful and sexy, and she felt it.

"You have such beautiful big blue eyes you know," I whispered to her softly. We kissed passionately as we rolled over, changing positions, now both naked.

As the night went by, we kissed, hugged, moaned, and just forgot about the rest of the world. Then we just held each other. It was as though, if either one of us let go of the other, we would fall off the face of the earth.

I was void of tension and feeling pretty good about myself and the woman that was by my side.

Samantha had been my salvation and I felt once more, this woman had saved my life. I looked down at her, sleeping naked with just a smile on her face. I was happy about what I saw. Feeling peaceful, I laid my head down next to her, closed my eyes, and fell off into a deep sleep.

I awoke to a bright sunny room, but the woman I had made love to the night before was gone. I stumbled out into the kitchen and saw it was all cleaned up from the dinner I had prepared for her. I dressed and made my way back up the hill to the main farmhouse.

In the kitchen was Samantha and Douglas, who had driven back to the farmhouse that morning from Washington D.C. They were sipping on coffee when I entered the room. Samantha stood up and fixed me a cup of coffee and said, “Good morning sleepy head.”

Not more than a minute later, they were joined at the table by Teresa, in her wheelchair, and Justin.

I sipped my coffee as I sat down next to Samantha. Breakfast consisted of fast-food sausage and egg biscuits, brought to the farmhouse by Douglas. He had picked up a bunch while getting gas at the local gas station. Within minutes, they were all devoured by the hungry crew.

Douglas looked up at me and asked, “Where is Spider?”

“He's chained up in the basement,” I responded.

“Well, we better get him some food and water, or he’ll die before we have a chance to interrogate him,” Douglas said.

“You’re right. Don’t want him to die before we have a chance to kill him,” I laughed.

Samantha laughed but saw I was not joking. “You wouldn’t do that, would you?” she asked.

"Of course not," I answered. "That would be too good for him."

We began to clean up when I asked Samantha if she'd take a walk with me. She agreed, and within moments, we were walking down the driveway and out along the countryside.

"Samantha," I began. "I want to apologize for last night," I said. "I don't want you to think I took advantage of you. I think what happened between us was an emotional thing, and I think there is some chemistry between us."

"Some chemistry?" she said in a raised voice. "I think it's more than just some chemistry," she quickly replied. "What happened last night was beautiful. It was two people who have feelings for each other, sharing those feelings," she said to me as she stopped walking and looked me straight in the eye.

"I know," I said to her. "That's why I think we need to put some distance between us for a while. I really care for you, and I can feel you really care for me. But I don't want to have happen to you, what happened to Christine," I continued.

"What are you saying, Jason?" she asked.

"I need to get Dylan and I need to go after the *KOF*," I said to her. "They are going to kill my friend and they're going to destroy our country if they're not stopped," I said as I held her by both arms.

"Within the next day or two, we will raid Granger's townhouse, and who knows what will happen there," I continued. "And we are getting close to bringing their entire organization down, but I'm afraid to get much closer to you, knowing they may come after you to get to me.

"They will do what they can to try and stop me, and I don't want you in the middle of all this," I said.

"I thought we were a thing," she said. "We made love last night," she continued. "I can't believe I was wrong about you," she said as she began to tear up.

"Samantha, we are a thing. I care about you. And last night was awesome. That's why we need to put some distance between us now. I don't want anything to happen to you. You know I couldn't handle it if something bad happened to you," I said.

"Will I see you again?" she asked trying to understand what I was saying.

"Yes, once this is behind us. Right now, I need to focus on saving Dylan and I refuse to jeopardize your life because of my needs," I responded to her. "That's why I asked Justin to come down, so he could care for Teresa."

"I understand," she said. "But take a look at what you're doing Jason," she continued. "You're doing exactly what you did with Christine. You're putting the saving of the world before us, and that's exactly what you did when you were younger," she said.

I was taken back by what she said. And I knew she was right.

"Well, okay then," she said in a hurting way. "You know where to find me once all this is done," she continued as she turned and headed back toward the main house. "I hope you'll stay in touch with me, so I won't worry," she shouted back at me, "but I won't wait forever for you," she said in an upset voice as she stormed back up the hill.

When I got back to the house, Samantha was packing up her things. "Douglas will be heading back to Washington later today, so

I'll have him drop me off back at the base," she said to me.

Chapter 41 – Ratification

Granger was awakened early in the morning and told it finally happened. Obtaining approval from three-fourths of the States to ratify the amendments was achieved. The USSA is about to become a reality.

Hearing the good news, he went down to the basement and pulled a folder from his desk that read: "The Creation of the United Southern States of America."

The documents inside only needed Bill McPherson's signature to become official. It was the establishment of a new Union-of-States from the eleven states that were ready to secede from the United States of America.

The document which Granger personally walked over to Bill McPherson's office for signing authorized eleven states, *(Alabama, Florida, Georgia, Louisiana, Mississippi, Texas, Arkansas, North and South Carolina, Tennessee, and Virginia),* to secede from the country known as The United States of America and would become part of the new

Union-of-States known as The United Southern States of America.

The document further stated that the Capital of the USSA would be Nashville, Tennessee and that the eleven states would be represented by his newly formed government.

Granger and Bill McPherson brought the document into a hastily called news conference in the White House briefing room and signed the papers in front of the cameras for the entire country to see. It was now official.

And as previously agreed upon, Granger Adams would become the constitutional author of this new Union-of-States. He would be given ninety days to draft the union's new constitution. In the meantime, the newly amended U.S. Constitution would serve as its legally binding rule of law.

Granger gracefully accepted the President's confidence in him and made it clear the task now upon him would be completed within the required timeframe. He then made copies of the signed document available to all attending press.

It wasn't until the next day that the press was able to fully disseminate the details to the American public and the rest of the world.

Reaction was immediate but for separate reasons. Most Americans applauded the news of splitting the United States Government into two separate entities. The overwhelming consensus was that it would now be able to better manage the needs of the country. They were certainly in favor of smaller government and they backed this approach as the solution to that goal.

There was also a positive response from various groups that migrated here from other countries. Muslims knew of the arrangement between Granger Adams and the New Muslim World Order. They couldn't wait to make the pilgrimage to Haram, their new State within the United Southern States of America. Finally, they thought. A homeland they could call their own. They felt if the Jews could have Israel, they could have Haram.

Outside of the country, the applause was noticeably lacking. Our ally countries were concerned the United States would now be a weakened nation, with less world power and influence. For years, they expected the United States to be the police force of the world. This allowed our allies to spend less on world stability and more on their own countries. They didn't care that the United States would eventually go broke having to pay for a secure world.

Those countries that wanted to destroy America were happy and saw this as an opportunity to finally take down the free-world giant.

Most importantly, however, the other two players in the trifecta of oil nations wanted to know who would be calling the shots when it came to management of the world's oil.

In the past, the United States President wielded the power along with Saudi Arabia and China. Now, they wanted to know if control would remain with the America they had been dealing with for the past five decades. But, if not, would there be two United States Presidents?

This further complicated the situation, as the world wondered which America should they listen to. This new split America was going to cause big changes in who controlled the world's economy. And sitting on the sidelines was Russia and several South American countries. Both Russia and Venezuela were willing bodies to step in and take control of the reins.

It was clear to me I had to take care of Granger Adams. I just hoped it wasn't too late. I couldn't let my country remain two nations, and I couldn't let those photos I gave to Granger Adams become public and ruin the legacy of my dear friend.

Chapter 42 – Back to Loyalty Road

Before heading to Nashville, Granger had decided to personally lead a force to Leesburg, Virginia, with the sole purpose of eliminating his arch enemy, Jason Williams.

Following the signals from the tracking device they planted into the back of Spider Webb's head, Granger directed an army of men to the Leesburg farmhouse that sat at the bottom of the hill on Loyalty Road. There was no sign of life at the smaller farmhouse further up the hill which he had learned was theirs as well. But there was smoke coming from the chimney at the large farmhouse down the hill.

Just under a hundred militia, fifty national guard soldiers, and twenty police officers surrounded the lower farmhouse. They slowly approached the large walk-around front porch with their guns drawn. They had orders to shoot-to-kill if anything moved.

From the center of the approaching army, a rather large bullhorn blasted out the words, "You have one minute to come out with your hands up and no one will get hurt. If you don't come out with your hands up, the house will be leveled to the ground."

It reminded some of the massacre in Waco, Texas some 35 years ago. The Waco siege of a compound belonging to the Branch Davidians, carried out by Federal and State law enforcement, as well as the U.S. military in early 1993, became a worldwide disgrace. Some felt this was going to be a repeat of that.

The words coming from the bullhorn had no effect, however, as the silence was deafening, and the new President of the USSA was starting to really get pissed off. He ordered the men to open fire on the farmhouse and take no prisoners. He wasn't going to take a chance Jason Williams escaped his grasp again.

His army of over a hundred opened fire, putting over three-thousand rounds of spent ammunition into the large two-story wooden house. All its windows, doors and much of the furniture on the front porch, as well as inside the farmhouse, were all destroyed by bullets.

When the firing stopped, Granger ordered his men to advance. His army approached the farmhouse, feeling safe no one could have survived that barrage of firepower. He ordered his militiamen into the house with guns drawn just in case anyone was still alive.

After all rooms were cleared, Granger advanced into the farmhouse to assess things for himself. Seeing no sign of bodies, he commanded his men to the basement where he hoped he would find the man he came for.

Searching the basement, they hollered to Granger Adams to come down and examine a box that was sitting in the middle of the empty basement and was addressed to him. When Granger made his way downstairs into the basement, he approached the box,

On top of the box, they found the tracking device that had been planted in Spider Webb's head just behind the ear. It was the only clue that indicated Jason Williams had ever been present at this location.

Granger opened the box and reached into it. He raised his hands and pulled out the head of Spider Webb. The head looked like it had been cut off with a dull kitchen knife. As Granger gasped for air to keep from passing out, he looked up and noticed Spider Webb's eyes were missing. Attached to the head was a note that read: *"You're next."*

Chapter 43 – Josef's Goal

**** Two days later ****

The United States of America was going through a difficult period after being split in two. There basically was a leadership crisis at hand, as two Presidents appeared to oversee things.

The President of Syria, Assam Bashula, was incredibly happy with the status of events. He knew the *KOF* was working out the details for the creation of a Muslim state in the middle of the country he hated, and his plans would soon come to fruition.

However, many other foreign Muslim leaders were becoming upset with President Assam Bashula's lack of action at what they felt was the perfect time to attack the infidels.

Terrorists from these other countries convinced a lone extremist, who lived in Dearborn, Michigan, to come out of the shadows and begin his own attacks. Their goal was to ensure the old America was surely crippled.

Josef Al-Hakim, who came to America three years ago, decided he was going to take charge of the situation and inflict major harm on the infidels that killed his family.

He was tall, dark and the spitting image of Osama Bin Laden, including the ragged clothes. Although Bin Laden had been killed many years ago, there were many in Dearborn that would stop and just stare.

Josef lived in a studio near Ford Woods Park in the heart of Dearborn, home to the largest Muslim population in the United States. Josef came to the United States after his parents were killed when he was just twenty years old. He gained access to the United States through a six-month visa that allowed him to visit his uncle in Dearborn. His uncle was a pilot for Delta Airlines, whose hub was in Dearborn.

While living with his uncle, he convinced many to join Al Qaeda and then ISIS. Once he was convinced of their loyalty to the Radical Islamic movement, he introduced them to the New Muslim World Order. All his recruits were loyal followers and interested in the NMWO's political plans and solutions.

Josef's goal in life was to destroy the old America. This was his obsession and his only purpose for living. The only thing he wanted from life was to revenge the death of his family who were killed in the retaliatory bombing directed by the current President of the United States, Bill McPherson.

Josef lost his father, mother and two brothers during a prayer session at midday, one of the five holy prayer times required by Allah. One of Bill McPherson's bombs landed in the courtyard of Al-Hakim's home and blew his family to pieces. He was running home to hustle them to safety but was two minutes too late.

While in Dearborn, Michigan, Josef studied avionics and electronics. During his three years here, he became very proficient at drone development and made a good living selling his drones on the internet and at fairs.

His first venture into the political arena was when he participated along with thousands of other Muslims in the march from the Karbala center in Warrendale to Ford Woods Park to mark the Arba'een, the 40th day after the death of Imam Hussain. The roar of the crowd excited him to the point where he knew his only goal was to kill.

Al-Hakim's most recent achievement was to build and control a drone that could fly at altitudes of five hundred feet and carry a two-pound weight which he could let drop on command. His excitement at this accomplishment was almost too much to control. He was also able to develop robot-like features that could respond to commands given from the ground.

Josef contacted Abdul Alhurra, a close friend who still lived in Iran, and requested he send Josef a few vials of the anthrax virus, to use in a test terrorist attack on the Americans.

Abdul worked at the University of Tehran, in the science and technology department, so obtaining virus samples was not a difficult task. The Iranians hid their chemical production plants from the West, under the disguise of their Nuclear plants. Workers were always shipping packages around the world and especially to Russia and to China.

It took only two weeks for the small FedEx package containing one vial of deadly anthrax virus to arrive at Josef's uncle's home.

It was the second Sunday in October, and the four drones he had now built were ready to fly and were ready to deliver their payload. The NFL football season was well underway and there was a home game scheduled in four surrounding cities he wanted to target.

Josef had driven all day and most of the night, sleeping only one night in a shady motel for $45, until he arrived in Foxboro, Massachusetts. He parked a few blocks away from Gillette Stadium and waited.

The stadium was over twenty years old and had replaced an even older Foxboro Stadium now torn down. Gillette Stadium was due to be replaced, and after what Josef Al-Hakim did today, they would need to expedite that effort.

Within half-an-hour after the singing of the Star-Spangled Banner, Josef opened the back door of his van and sent his drone skyward. A few minutes later, it was hovering over mid-field at Gillette Stadium.

Josef had recruited three young volunteers to fly three of the other drones on his command, which were nothing more than decoys, over the home stadiums of the New York Giants, the Washington Redskins, and the Buffalo Bills. He sent them off to their respective target cities and put them up in the finest hotels. Money was no object, as the NMWO was well financed, and had several banks within Muslim communities handling its financial needs. Josef's real target, however, was the New England Patriots because they carried the American symbol on their helmets.

The first three drones carried no payload. Their only role was to be part of the headline from the news media that several strange drones were observed flying over four northeast NFL stadiums which were filled with innocent men, women, and children.

However, the one he controlled over Gillette Stadium contained a motorized fan and the vial of anthrax virus.

The Pittsburgh Steelers were playing at Gillette Stadium at 1:00 P.M. and Josef was inside his white van parked a few blocks from the stadium. The large clear vial full of over half a million spores of the anthrax virus was attached to his drone, along with a small battery-operated fan that would be used to disperse the virus over the stadium at his command.

He didn't have to drop anything, and he didn't have to hope it exploded. He simply was going to remotely open the vial and allow the fan to blow chemicals over the stadium. This attack would result in a mass panic once they realized what was happening. Josef knew death would not be instant and the virus could be neutralized if those sickened by anthrax were given antibiotics within a couple of days. However, he knew many would die.

The inhaled form of the disease is a real threat in the hands of a bioterrorist. Anthrax can enter the body through the skin via a break in the skin like a cut or sore but inhaled through the nose or mouth it is the deadliest form of the virus.

He signaled his three recruits to release their drones and direct them over the NFL stadiums in Washington D.C., Buffalo, New York, and the Meadowlands Sports Complex in New Jersey which serves as the home stadium for two NFL franchises: The New York Giants and the New York Jets.

He received back notice from all three recruits that their drones were airborne within minutes. Hearing that, he called the FBI on a burner phone he had just purchased to inform authorities that there were four drones flying over several NFL stadiums.

Within seconds of doing that, he heard on the radio that the FBI and the DHS had issued an alert that all four NFL stadiums were to be evacuated immediately, due to some suspicious drones flying overhead.

Josef Al-Hakim had caused mass panic in the old United States of America and he was thrilled.

He pushed the red button on his controller which activated the remote-controlled fan on his drone. He then reached over and slid a lever on his controller which opened the vial containing the deadly anthrax virus. Within seconds, the powder contained in the vial was being spread over Gillette Stadium.

Thousands of football fans were running for exits and were trampling each other. Some, once they saw the drone flying overhead, jumped from the top of the stadium's wall. Those that jumped did not survive the fall.

There were many little children at the stadium and many others in wheelchairs, and all suffered as the mass crowd just ran over them. They stood no chance up against the panicked crowds running in any direction they could.

Josef knew his drones would soon be intercepted by DHS, FBI and local authorities and brought down by use of jamming signals, but he couldn't help but continue to watch as the deadly anthrax virus flew out onto the field spraying the tens of thousands of fans that were still in the stadium trying to get out. His plan had worked, and he was ecstatic.

A few minutes later, he shut down the drone and let it crash to the ground. He removed the chemical mask he was wearing, climbed up into the front seat of the white van and drove off into the sunset.

He knew the death toll would be significant and he was right. He was proud of his terrorist act against the country he so hated. He was proud he could claim this act for the New Muslim World Order.

Allah Akbar, he said over and over to himself during his ten-hour drive. Josef didn't stop until he reached a dingy motel just outside of Frederick, Maryland. It was midnight and he hadn't eaten anything all day. His only stops were to pray.

The next morning, having been awake for most of the night from the street noise of the fleabag motel he was staying in, he knew his next goal was to find a place to live in the Washington D.C. area. Someplace where he could eat and pray on a regular basis.

He checked out a room-for-rent he had found on the internet and settled into a one-bedroom third-floor attic apartment on Georgia Avenue, a few blocks west of Grant Circle. The place was near the First Hijra Muslim Community Center, so he could easily walk there several times a day to pray. Paying the first few months' rent in cash, Josef moved his few belongings in and settled down.

The effect of the anthrax virus that was dropped over Gillette Stadium was devastating. Thousands died and double that amount became ill. Hundreds of quarantine centers were set up to handle the disaster just outside of Foxboro. The government's report, however, indicated the illnesses were due to tainted food, and not an attack on our country by terrorists. Not many who were at the stadium were fooled by this false claim.

The FBI had received a tip from one of Josef's three volunteers and was able to trace back the information to Josef's uncle's house in Dearborn. There, they found a Geiger counter plus evidence some type of virus or bacteria had been present in the house. Since Josef knew nothing about dirty bombs, he just stored the Geiger counter he purchased online, in a closet. Unfortunately, he hadn't wiped his fingerprints from the device.

They added Josef's picture to the Bureau's ten most wanted list and began surveillance of his uncle's home in Dearborn, hoping Josef would return. They also added Josef to the TSA's no-fly list.

Chapter 44 – New Recruits

Josef attended prayer services at the Community Center every day.

During his first week there, he met a young Muslim and they quickly became friends. They both began attending prayer sessions together, five times a day. Jamal was just seventeen and lived with his parents in a two-bedroom row house. He was innocent looking, young, and impressionable.

Jamal looked up to Josef because he was wise and knew so much about the Koran. He would sit with Josef after their prayer sessions and talk about Josef's homeland, and how the Americans were destroying it. Jamal had asked Josef to teach him how to make bombs and detonators, and he was eager to learn. Josef had become quite the expert at radicalizing his fellow Muslims, simply by describing the terror of what Americans were doing to their homeland.

Josef Al-Hakim did not make Syria's President aware the capital city of the United States, Washington D.C., was going to be his next target. On his own, he had formulated a detailed plan for a double attack there that included both his new friend Jamal and his uncle, Omar Nazari.

Josef felt if President Bashula were aware of his latest plans, he would not be happy. President Bashula did not want anything to disrupt preparations that were now underway to establish a Caliphate within the United Southern States of America, even if it were only in a newly formed and not universally recognized Union-of-States.

Acting on his own, however, Josef planned two lone-wolf attacks on Washington D.C. The first attack would be carried out by Jamal, and his uncle Omar Nazari would complete the double whammy. Before sending his new friend out to his destiny, Josef packed up his belongings, purchased a used van from a neighbor and prepared to leave the area after these two attacks were completed.

He researched Muslim communities in Florida and had decided the central part of the State would be a good place to settle down for a while.

On the morning of the first attack, at approximately 10:00 A.M., Jamal drove Josef's old beat-up white van into the lower front entrance of the Ronald Reagan International Trade Center, which was located at 1300 Pennsylvania Avenue. The underground parking garage was just down the road from the White House and the Capitol Building.

Jamal, who soon would be one of Islam's martyrs, emerged from behind the wheel. "Do not anyone move," the Arabic-looking young man yelled to the crowd standing by the security booth. He raised his hand for everyone to stop in place.

"My name is Jamal, and I will blow this area to pieces if you do not stop moving," he said. The garage was full of tourists and attendants, as well as a handful of security guards.

Josef knew this terrorist act alone would cause more horror than the small amount of people killed by the blast. However, he knew many would die. He was happy Jamal had agreed to do this for him.

Jamal was holding what was believed to be a detonator. His thumb was on the red button at the top of the device he held. The security guards that were there to protect the complex froze. "Thank you," he said as he motioned everyone out into the open area.

"I have several thousand pounds of ammonium nitrate in the back of my van," he told them. "If I press this button, it will take out the entire parking garage. The explosion will leave a crater thirty feet deep and forty feet around. No one will ever find your bodies. Most of you will be blown apart or barbecued and the rest of you will lack arms and legs. So, I encourage you not to move.

"Today will go down in history as the day a double attack occurred on this nation's capital," he said. "This city is about to pay the price for what your President did to my friend's family three years ago," he told them. "I am here to avenge the deaths of his parents and his brothers," Jamal said, "so yes, you are about to die here."

With all eyes focused on Jamal's movement, in an instant, a shot was heard that caused everyone to freeze.

"*Allahu akbar,* in the name of Allah," Jamal shouted out. He then pressed the red button in the middle of the detonator as he fell to the ground.

The button clicked, and it appeared some type of mechanism was activated. Everyone stared at the white van, but nothing happened. As Jamal fell to the ground, the detonator dropped a few feet away from his side.

The shot, which was fired by a guard who was standing only a foot behind a column just behind the Muslim terrorist, went cleanly through the back of Jamal's head and out through his forehead.

The shot was clean but didn't bring instant death. Jamal had a moment to become a Martyr, where he would spend all eternity with his 72 virgins. Luckily, the asshole didn't know what he was doing and screwed up his dream. His incompetence, however, saved everyone on the grounds of the garage.

With Jamal dead on the floor of the underground parking garage, only Josef knew what was to happen next.

Chapter 45 – The Beginning of the End

Before leaving Dearborn, Josef was able to successfully radicalize his uncle Omar. He convinced him, a pilot of twenty years with Delta Airlines, to join him in his lone-wolf Jihadist activities.

Now gone from his uncle's home, Josef wasn't sure if he could count on his uncle to implement the terrorist attacks they had planned.

He decided to call his uncle and confirm plans for Omar's attack. Fearing the FBI or NSA would be listening in on Omar's phone calls, he left a coded fake message telling him his loan was approved and he should call the finance company to arrange a payment schedule.

Two hours later, he received a phone call from Omar letting him know he was ready to serve Allah. He told Josef he would be in Atlanta tomorrow morning and was scheduled to fly to Dulles Airport, just outside of Washington D.C. around noon that same day.

Omar indicated he would then be on to Kennedy airport in New York City shortly after that. Omar told Josef he would see him again in heaven.

The next morning, Omar began what would be his last scheduled workday with Delta Airlines. He lifted his Delta 777 off the ground from Atlanta's Hartsfield Airport and headed to Dulles airport outside of Washington, D.C.

After an hour layover at Dulles Airport, Omar was finally cleared for takeoff, as he piloted his Delta 777 east, out over the Atlantic Ocean on a flight headed for New York City. His planned flight to New York, however, was about to be converted into a second attack that would stun the nation and rally Muslims all over the world. Today was the day he was going to die and be received by Allah as his reward.

The aging Delta 777 Jetliner, with 290 passengers and 8 crew members including the pilot, continued east for about fifteen minutes. At this point, Omar locked the cabin door from inside. He'd already slashed the throats of his co-pilot, who was now slumped over in her seat, and his navigator, who was lying on the cabin floor. He announced to the passengers and crew the aircraft had experienced a minor electrical failure and they were returning to Dulles Airport for an emergency maintenance repair.

He calmed everyone down by telling them the problem was not serious, but FAA regulation prohibited him from continuing with his flight plan. The landing would be routine, and he told them he didn't expect to be on the ground for more than fifteen minutes.

He let the flight crew know the electrical problem was with the cabin door and it had locked shut with no method of opening it. He urged the crew to keep the passengers calm, and that they'd be on the ground within the next few minutes.

Omar knew they would all be dead within the next few minutes. Either their plane would be shot down by the National Guard's F-16's for entering prohibited airspace, or they would all praise Allah as they made history by crashing into the building located at 1600 Pennsylvania Ave.

He was aware even if these F-16's immediately took off from Andrews Air Force

Base, just 10 miles from the White House, they would not get to his location in time to prevent his plane from crashing into the home of the President of the United States, an event that would rally the entire Arab world.

The question that ran through his mind was, should he kill almost 300 innocent people and cause the United States of America to retaliate against Syria, possibly eliminating it from the face of the earth. Or should he plan to surrender himself to the infidels and return the plane safely back to Dulles Airport.

Now less than one hundred miles from the coastline of the United States, he was nervous and scared, but completely in charge of his wits. All he kept thinking about was the 72 virgins he would meet up with later.

"Flight 8883, please come in," he heard over his radio. "Request you correct your course immediately as you are beginning to enter restricted airspace over Washington D.C. Please come in flight 8883," the flight controller said.

There was no response from Omar Nazari, who knew he was not off-course. He also knew if he responded, it would mean certain death if he did not correct his current course immediately.

What Omar did do, however, was broadcast a Mayday call indicating he was having electrical problems and they were heading back to Dulles Airport for an emergency landing. He knew this would buy him a few minutes to make his final decision.

"Flight 8883," the control tower could be heard saying again. "You are now in restricted airspace. Two National Guard F-16's jets have been launched from Andrews Air Force base, and you only have a few moments to correct course before they shoot you down. Do you read?" the controllers voice could be heard yelling over the radio.

Omar responded to the control tower in Arabic, as the Delta 777 approached within 30 miles of the coastline and the White House.

The End

Epilogue

Before the United-Six could stage a rescue attempt, on a day that would go down in history, Dylan Rains was unchained, brought to his feet, and loaded into the SUV parked in Granger Adams' townhouse garage.

Granger Adams, General Garrett Johnson, and their one-legged prisoner then made the ten-minute trip to the White House where Dylan Rains was taken to be further interrogated and prepped for his journey down to Guantanamo Bay, Cuba.

They were unaware that Flight 8883 had just taken off from Dulles Airport, in what would be its final flight.

WHERE ARE THEY NOW?

Bill McPherson:

Serving a second term as President of the United States, he was facing enormous pressure from Congress and the people of his country to respond to the latest terrorist attacks on American soil ~~ attacks that killed many and caused the country to fear their personal freedom was under attack.

He also knew his long-time friend was closing in on ***The Knights of Freedom*** and he would have to decide where his loyalties lay.

Douglas Williams:

Vice President of the United States, Douglas Williams had infiltrated the ***KOF*** and provided his brother Jason with detailed information about the organization's membership, plans, finances, weaknesses, and strengths. This was not going unnoticed by ***The Knights of Freedom***.

Luckily, what was going unnoticed was that Douglas and The United-Six were preparing an attack on Granger Adams' townhouse, in an attempt to rescue Dylan Rains. They were unaware he had been moved.

General Garrett Johnson:

General Garrett Johnson continues to be President McPherson's Chief-of-Staff. He is not happy about his partner-in-crime, Granger Adams, and his plan to allow a Caliphate for Muslims inside the United Southern States of America. Garrett wants his partner eliminated.

Granger Adams:

Granger Adams continues to head up the subversive group known as ***The Knights of Freedom***. He has just completed his life-long goal to establish a new Union-of-States, known as the United Southern States of America.

Due to his killing rampage, however, he has acquired a growing list of enemies and they are beginning to close in on him.

Teresa Williams:

Teresa Williams has all but destroyed her relationship with her father. She has amends to make and whether she can make this happen, is yet to be seen. She has, however, taken the first step in rebuilding that relationship.

Samantha Wilkinson:

Samantha is saddened by what she thought was a blossoming relationship with her friend and past patient Jason Williams. She feels his loyalty to his country means more to him than his feelings for her.

She is also worried he is doing exactly what he vowed never to do again and that is to put his loyalty to his country over his personal life. Was this deja vu for Jason Williams?

Omar Nazari:

He is the uncle of Josef Al-Hakim and was radicalized by his nephew. A pilot for Delta Airlines, he has agreed to help Josef avenge the death of his family three years ago by carrying out a deadly terrorist attack in Washington D.C.

Josef Al-Hakim:

Confident his drones will perform, Josef is making plans to build a small manufacturing plant with the goal of building several hundred drones.

He also has plans to construct several distribution centers in six other states where he'll have these drones mounted with their payload. Then these distribution centers will be the release points for his chemical attack on the U.S.

Jason Williams:

Jason has been through a lot and learned a great deal about himself. However, he realized he is again giving up everything important in his life to save the country he loves. He wants to do what is right but is not sure what that is.

Dylan Rains:

Dylan has been held captive by ***The Knights of Freedom*** for over a week and has just been moved to the White House for further interrogation and an eventual journey to Guantanamo Bay, Cuba. As of now, there are no planned negotiations for his release.

The Knights of Freedom:

Although this organization has achieved its goal of splitting the United States of America into two nations, its followers are concerned that the lack of order that exists in the country over the mayhem it has caused may send the reign of this organization into a tailspin.

At the ***KOF*** Capital of The United Southern States of America, they are quickly working on the creation of their twelfth state, "Haram". There is discussion over its location within the other eleven states of the USSA.

Look for Book III in this Trilogy

"The Winds of Change"